ADA

Ada Moncrieff is the author of *Murder Most Festive* and *Murder at the Theatre Royal*. She lives and works in London.

ADA MONCRIEFF

Murder at Maybridge Castle

VINTAGE

3 5 7 9 10 8 6 4

Vintage is part of the Penguin Random House group of companies
whose addresses can be found at global.penguinrandomhouse.com

Penguin
Random House
UK

First published by Vintage in 2023

penguin.co.uk/vintage

Typeset in 11/15.75pt Stempel Garamond LT Std
by Jouve (UK), Milton Keynes.
Printed and bound in Great Britain by Clays Ltd, Elcograf S.p.A.

The authorised representative in the EEA is Penguin Random House
Ireland, Morrison Chambers, 32 Nassau Street, Dublin D02 YH68

A CIP catalogue record for this book is available from the British Library

ISBN 9781787304314

Penguin Random House is committed to a sustainable future
for our business, our readers and our planet. This book is made
from Forest Stewardship Council® certified paper.

Cast of Characters

Mr Archibald (the Moores' previous employer)

Eleanor Beaumont – avid follower of all things Spiritualist, recently married to Dr John Beaumont

Dr John Beaumont – GP in the suburbs of London

Constable Crookshank

Margery Dawson

Inspector Forsythe

Raymond Hammond – insurance man with an interest in the supernatural

Kenneth Hammond – son of Raymond Hammond, philosophy student

Lord and Lady Holmcroft

Charles Howton – owner of Maybridge Castle

Daphne King – former agony columnist, now investigative reporter for the *Chronicle* newspaper

Veronica

Alice Macauley

Madame Marla and Madame Thelma

Dr Mayfield

Mr Moore – Charles Howton's valet-cum-butler-cum-handyman

Mrs Moore – cook and housekeeper at Maybridge Castle, married to Mr Moore

Helena Rackham – old friend of Charles Howton, academic at Edinburgh University specialising in studies into witchcraft

Winifred Roberts – acquaintance of Charles Howton, socialite in London and hotel correspondent for *Town and Country* magazine

the Reverend St John Smith

Jim Sullivan

Mrs Amelia Thewley – renowned in Spiritualist circles as a sceptic and debunker, enjoys travelling far and wide with her cat, Duke

1

The invitations had all arrived with their recipients the same day: 15 November 1936. Thick cream envelopes trimmed with a red border, a heavy, extravagant wax seal affixed to each one. Indistinct at first, on closer inspection the seal was revealed to be a bat. Indeed, each envelope had flitted and fluttered its way into the homes of the invitees with all the precision of a bat swooping to its prey at dusk. Names and addresses written in a spidery cursive, the envelopes were sliced, prised and torn open to reveal their contents. Contents which tantalised and teased: an invitation to spend three nights at Maybridge Castle.

Four weeks had passed since then. Four weeks during which Christmas trees had been hauled through snowy streets, baubles arranged meticulously. Trinkets had been purchased, though not yet wrapped. Socks had been knitted for great-nieces and great-nephews, Christmas puddings had been stirred and set. Now, the day of departure had arrived. It was 15 December, and a week-end at Maybridge Castle lay ahead. For most, the three nights presented a thrilling proposition. For some, other concerns and preoccupations nagged and niggled. For all of the guests, the weekend would prove to have consequences beyond anyone's imaginings.

The kettle was whistling in the London suburb of Surbiton as Eleanor Beaumont attempted to close her suitcase for the third time. She had already sacrificed two jumpers and three blouses. She had to bring the necessary ensembles to impress the other guests.

'Oh, John,' called Eleanor as she trotted to the door, 'do be a dear and see to the kettle, will you?'

The kettle had also been whistling the day that the invitation had arrived all those weeks ago. Eleanor Beaumont, recently married and even more recently turned twenty-five, saw it as one of her prized domestic duties to hurry for the morning post. She thought back to that day. The day where everything had changed.

The postman had emitted an embarrassing shriek when his delivery had been snatched from his hands, the envelopes barely through the letterbox to number 17, Canterbury Road, Surbiton.

Eleanor had examined the day's missives. One letter addressed to Dr John Beaumont – plain, a cheap envelope, dull block capitals. She'd frowned and slipped it into the pocket of her apron before turning her attention to the other envelope. Her eyes had widened, her thin black eyebrows telegraphing delight and surprise. No, it couldn't be. Could it? Involuntarily, her tongue flicked from her mouth in a gesture of concentration one would ordinarily associate with a toddler's face as they attempted to smear jam on wallpaper.

'Everything all right, darling?' John called wearily from the kitchen. 'Remind me: where do we keep the sugar?'

Eleanor patted the envelope in her pocket and held the other before her as if offering it in sacrifice to the gods of fortune. A warmth had spread through her body. She hadn't dared to dream that this day would come. With measured steps, she paced along the carpeted hallway and returned to the kitchen. Still holding the envelope aloft, she swooped up a kitchen rag and dried the few splashes of tea that were evidence of her husband's attempts to have the brew ready for her.

John leant against the kitchen counter expectantly, a teaspoon in his left hand.

'Top right-hand cupboard,' murmured Eleanor, glancing at her husband only fleetingly. 'John – I – think you ought to sit down.'

Her husband frowned and adjusted his tie. Even on his days off from the general practice, John insisted on wearing his ironed trousers, starched shirt and a tie – today, it was green.

Eleanor reached for a knife from the cutlery drawer and slowly, ever so slowly, opened the envelope. John watched in bemusement as she carefully drew out a letter and her eyes danced over the lines. Eleanor's face lit in a grin and she began waving the letter at her husband.

'This is it!' she squealed, jigging excitedly in her slippers. 'Every day for two months I've prayed for this!'

John was more baffled than before. 'Darling, I'm entirely in the dark here: what on earth is going on?'

Eleanor took a deep breath. She hadn't told her husband about this. She hadn't wanted to excite him. Or, rather, alarm him. The moment had, however, arrived. She would have to reveal all.

'It's – it's . . .' she began, but could barely get her words out. 'I've won! We've won!'

His understanding far from growing, John insisted that his wife sit at the table, take a sip of her tea and explain quite what had got her into this state of elation.

'John, dearest, I wanted to surprise you,' Eleanor explained. This, however, was not strictly true. This was not, despite her best attempts at dressing it up to the contrary, a surprise treat for her husband. It was a dream of hers. 'There was a competition – in *Spiritualism Now*.'

John immediately treated his wife to a mock eye-roll. Though their union and their household were both relatively new – the wedding photo upon their mantelpiece had been taken only three months earlier, in August – this was a routine that they had settled into with comforting ease: Eleanor mentioned her favourite publication, the fortnightly magazine dedicated to the practice of modern Spiritualism, and her husband indulged in exaggerated and ostentatious snobbery about it.

'I had to write in, explaining why I ought to win – why we ought to win,' Eleanor continued, her tea growing cold. 'And bob's your uncle – he's said that I was the best – the – the most deserving!'

It took two custard creams and John's hand upon his wife's for the entire story to emerge coherently. Eleanor Beaumont – Mrs Eleanor Beaumont, if you please – had been awarded a three-night stay at England's most exciting new hotel (among readers of *Spiritualism Now*, John qualified quietly): Maybridge Castle, the country's first haunted hotel.

John glanced at the last paragraph of the letter that his wife had finally laid down upon the table.

> *. . . your letter struck a chord with me, Mrs Beaumont, and I heartily look forward to welcoming you and your husband to our not*

*terribly humble abode. Maybridge Castle, as well
as our spectral residents and our medium
associates, Madame Thelma and Madame Marla,
eagerly await your arrival on 15 December.*

*Your fellow traveller on the road to other-
worldly enlightenment,*

Charles Howton

Eleanor's reverie was interrupted by her husband as
he entered the bedroom carrying two steaming cups
of tea.

'Oh, you're an angel, John,' she said as she accepted
hers. 'Now be a dear and sit on this suitcase, will you? I
can't leave any more of these blouses behind. I simply
shan't!'

'The taxi's coming in ten minutes, Kenneth. It's taking
me to the station – and I sincerely hope that it'll be
taking you as well,' Raymond Hammond said evenly to
his son. Their bags were packed, their coats were on.
Raymond had thought the tantrums were over. His son,
Kenneth, had other ideas.

'I still don't understand. Why the bloody hell would
you want to go there, Pa? Why the bloody hell do you
continue to see that bloody man?'

Kenneth Hammond swept back his hair with one hand

and balled the other into a tight fist. His father was accustomed to his outbursts. Ever since he was a child (ever since the age of five, to be as painfully precise as possible, his father often observed), Kenneth had been prone to tantrums. Heartbreakingly inconsolable at best, dangerously volatile at worst, Kenneth's episodes had, for the last fourteen years, defined and ruled his father's life.

Raymond knew himself to be a kind father. An understanding man, he had done his utmost to keep his son on an even keel. Placated him when he needed placating, allowing him space to pace and rant when the time came. He was proud of the way in which he, Raymond Hammond, a man who had worked in insurance for the last forty years without ever once suggesting to his employers that he might be capable of more than reliable pen-pushing, had raised this intelligent, passionate, headstrong young man. And single-handed, at that.

Kenneth stared through the window in their living room. The living room that Raymond had been occupying in solitude since his son had gone to read philosophy at Cambridge last year. Kenneth snorted in derision once more and snatched the letter from the side table where it had been lying for four weeks.

'"*Wishing that it may bring you some peace, Charles.*"' Kenneth spat in anger. 'How dare he? How bloody dare he?'

Calmly, Raymond approached his son. With a gentle smile, he took the letter – already slightly crumpled from Kenneth's grip – and folded it. 'He means well, son. And let's ease up on the fire and brimstone, eh? Quite enough "bloodys" for a Friday morning, wouldn't you say? It's only three nights – we'll be back here on Monday.'

Kenneth's nostrils flared and he once more sprang to his feet. 'Three nights, three months, three seconds – it doesn't matter how long the trip is. It's the principle of the thing. Don't be so naive, Pa. He doesn't mean well. He means to do right by one person and one person only: Charles bloody Howton.'

Raymond began fastening the buttons on his mustard cardigan. He loved his son, desperately so, and he had learnt that Kenneth's tempers could often only be doused with patience and a weary smile.

'Charles bloody Howton is one of my dearest, oldest friends,' Raymond said, placing a hand on his son's tensed arm. 'He is, of course, aware of my interest in such pursuits as these . . . I make no secret of my curiosity about the occult and that, as you call it, hokum and balderdash. He's been so kind as to invite me to this Maybridge Castle of his – what possible harm could come of accepting?'

As soon as the utterance left his mouth, Raymond

realised the error that he had made. His choice of words were like a red rag to a bull. Immediate action would be required in order to avert instant disaster. 'Kenneth – please, do an old man an act of charity. You promised you'd come with me? Cumbria's a long, long way from Cambridge – it'll do you good, clear your head, get those cobwebs truly blown away before Christmas. What say we make an adventure of it?'

'I know perfectly well where Cumbria is,' Kenneth blurted bitterly, his eyes narrowed.

'Son – please.' The quiver in his voice surprised even Raymond himself. It seemed to soften his son, who sighed deeply.

'Fine. I'll come,' Kenneth relented. 'P'raps you're right: a bit of a breather after Michaelmas term might do me the world of good. Some fresh air to reinvigorate the soul after all that Schopenhauer. But I won't indulge that Howton man. Over my dead body will I indulge that man.'

Helena Rackham glanced at the clock. Eight fifteen. She would need to leave her study in the next half an hour if she was to make the train from Edinburgh to Asperdale.

She could have taken an earlier one, of course. Even travelled yesterday evening. But there were a few final

9

books she had wanted to take out from the university library.

Her travel bag, modest in size, sat in the corner of her college study. She went to her coat and patted its pockets: train ticket, Christmas card, reading glasses and invitation.

She took this last item from her pocket and smiled at the letter. Charles was a charmer. Always had been. She traced her fingers over the handwriting. This hadn't been the first draft. Charles would have practised several iterations of this invitation. Perhaps the first version had been playful with a hint of self-deprecation. Yes, that would be Charles's first instinct. The second draft, a touch more serious. He might have used his battered old thesaurus to add a drop of colour to his vocabulary choices. There would have been some crossings-out, naturally – countless crossings-out, if Helena knew her dear old friend Charles. The third version, that would be where it had cohered. The jaunty and the portentous, the levity and the self-assurance.

Of course he needn't have put in such effort, Helena reflected as she dipped a digestive into her tea and swirled it ruminatively. She glanced out of her study window at the cobbled streets of Edinburgh below. Students were milling about already, scarves tightened, breath fogging before them. She had no lectures today,

Fridays being her one solid day away from the eager young minds that usually sat enraptured by her lessons on the other days of the week. No, Fridays were just for her. For her and her writing. Although goodness knew that the writing had hit something of a halt of late. Her usual vim and vigour was depleted. Which was why Charles's invitation required minimal consideration. It was just the thing to reinvigorate her, rev up those once-whirring engines of thought and academic insight that had made her reputation as Britain's foremost scholar of the history of the witch-hunts.

She re-read the most teasingly appealing part of the letter.

> . . . *of course, you'll be the first – the very first – academic to set foot upon it. Lord knows what you might find – aside from a cursed rabbit's paw and a rotting witch's hat, of course. In all seriousness, Helena, how could I allow anyone else to poke their nose into this? A burial ground for witches, here on the very property that your dearest darling Charlie snapped up only a year ago. It's fate. Destiny. The gods – or rather, goddesses – have decreed it. You simply must come – 15 December. There'll be others here, naturally, as I thought your little academic investigation would coincide*

*rather deliciously with our grand opening. I'm
well aware of your aversion to the exigencies of
social gatherings, but what's a hotel sans a motley
assortment of guests whose paths shall cross once
and once only?*

*PS – the trains from Edinburgh are awfully cheap.
No excuses, Helena.*

She smiled to herself. It would be quite the boon, an
irresistible expedition to revivify her academic enthusiasm. Who knew what she might find? And as for the
motley assortment of guests – Helena rather bristled at
the thought of spending three nights in the company of
strangers. But if their paths were only to cross this once,
then it was a trial that Helena Rackham could withstand.
Of that, she was certain.

Winifred Roberts twisted the sapphire ring on her forefinger. An heirloom from her grandmother, the ring's
rotations had always signified Winifred's excitement.
And by golly was Winifred excited. She would never
dream of letting on, naturally. No, that would be far
too . . . vulgar. The invitation had piqued her interest the
second it had arrived, and now, four weeks later, she was

ready to go and see what silly old Charles Howton had been up to in the wilds of Cumbria.

The train journey there would give her the chance to finish that potboiler she'd been reading. And she had a first-class ticket, so no danger of being sat next to someone munching a pickled egg sandwich. Winifred glanced in the mirror hanging above the mantelpiece in her living room. She was ready to make a splash up there in deepest, darkest Cumbria.

The fact of the matter was that she was bored of London. Bored of the monotonous merry-go-round of dry parties attended by the same dry denizens of so-called high society. Years ago, she had affected this boredom. It was fashionable. Nonchalance in the face of vintage champagne at the Savoy in the company of minor royalty from Luxembourg. A shrug of the shoulders when invited for vol-au-vents and a shooting weekend in the Suffolk pile of some insufferable aristocrat or other. Of course, insufferable aristocrats had their time and their place. But, with a regularity that left her confounded, Winifred was finding herself wishing that both time and place were as far away from her as possible. Baronet So-and-So, Lady Twiddle-thumbs – they all had the same dreary things to say, the same tired witticisms to trot out, and the same decades-old anecdotes to roll before her. Yes, she had heard about the butler who had swallowed the pearls. Wasn't it an outrage! And yes, she agreed that the caviar at the DuBelvoirs' soiree in June was quite substandard.

None of it mattered. Winifred Roberts had worked tirelessly for years now to ascend to her place among the hierarchy of London. As *Town and Country*'s prestigious hotel correspondent, she was invited to all of the most coveted events in town. But how tired of it she was. Just thinking of it prompted a yawn as she reclined in the conservatory of her small house in Richmond.

This time a year ago, she would never have entertained anything as ludicrous as the invitation that she had retrieved from her doormat that morning. Such a very, very ludicrous invitation. A haunted hotel? In December? A highly coveted *weekend* in December? And in *the North* of all places? From Charles "flying by the seat of his slacks" Howton? Charles "suave as a Rolls Royce, reliable as a decommissioned tractor" Howton? No, the Winifred of December 1935 would have ripped it to shreds while laughing, possibly before pouring herself another glass of champagne.

But the Winifred of December 1936 found the invitation oddly compelling. Champagne may have lost its allure for her, but the opportunity to witness first-hand Charles Howton's latest escapade certainly had not.

She plucked the invitation from the handbag that she had slung on to the back of her armchair and turned it over in her immaculately manicured hands.

. . . Maybridge Castle is it for me, Winifred. The Charles of old is no more. What that gadabout knew about a sound investment, one could write on the back of a postage stamp. In fact, one would be hard pressed to fill the back of a postage stamp with what the old Charles Howton knew about a sound investment. This is the one. And I need you to spread the word about it. Give us a sparkling review in your mellifluous prose – paint a picture that will have the guests flocking to Maybridge Castle. If not for the opportunity to converse with their dearly departed, then at least for the opportunity to sample some of Mrs Moore's drop scones and rock buns. Quite the treasure of a housekeeper I've bagged there, I can tell you. In any case, I find myself digressing. Old habits and what have you. Please excise anything else taking up space in your diary: 15 December 1936, the day Winifred Roberts arrives for a three-day sojourn at

England's most breath-taking, jaw-dropping,
soul-shaking new hotel.
   Shan't take no for an answer,
   Charles xx

Winifred looked out at the small unkempt garden that she had neglected in the three years since living in Richmond. It was full of frosty weeds, and a fox cantered across the ice on the lichen-stained paving stones, entirely unmoved by the proximity to a human dwelling. Christmas this year was looking to be an uneventful affair. There were, of course, the usual rounds to be made: Claridge's, the Ritz, perhaps an overnighter at Cliveden. All as polished to dull perfection as ever. Maybridge Castle, however, promised to be a far more interesting stay. A lark to see what a mess Charles would make of the place, what gaggle of eccentrics and curios he would gather about him for the grand opening. Winifred placed her delicate teacup back in its saucer. She never could resist watching someone hurtling headlong into catastrophe.

Mrs Amelia Thewley opened her wardrobe door. The grey cardigan, that would have to come. No need for too many blouses: it was only a three-night stay. Thermals, without doubt. In her seventy-five years, she had experienced enough English winters to know that the secret to success is layers. Long-sleeved, followed by short-sleeved, and possibly another long-sleeved before one's cardigan. And then of course one's coat. The ermine collar of Mrs Thewley's coat negated the need for a scarf, and she could never be doing with the fussing and kerfuffle necessitated by such an unwieldy accoutrement. She enjoyed thinking of herself as one of those millefeuilles she had enjoyed with her husband Arthur back in Paris when one century was giving way to the next.

Tights, naturally. Some sturdy boots in case there was treacherous terrain to be traversed. House-slippers. Her lace-up Derby shoes. She had already inventoried the necessaries for her toilette. She had carried out this laborious task the night before her journey, knowing that her various potions and ointments would require several hours of packing.

Downstairs, she had tidied up the pine needles that had already fallen from her Christmas tree, and had neatly arranged two stockings above the hearth. Hers was a bright red colour with a gold 'A' stitched along the front, while Duke's was a forest green with a silver 'D'.

'And we'll bring your basket, don't fret, Duke,' Mrs Thewley declared in the sing-song tones she reserved for reassuring her tabby cat in circumstances that provoked anxiety. 'I might even sneak in a few of your special turkey treats, nearly Christmas after all. Although, that said, we'll be back on Monday morning – mightn't do you any harm to abstain from gobbling down those morsels for one weekend suppose.'

Mrs Thewley poked Duke's not insubstantial tummy. In response, Duke, slightly portly in his old age but no less nimble than when he was a kitten, slunk around her legs and yawned.

'Bored, are we, young sir?' Mrs Thewley tutted. 'Well, I shall have to see to it that Mr Charles Howton lays on a most eventful itinerary for us. Let's not cause too much trouble this time, eh?'

At this, Duke meowed lightly in agreement. Mrs Thewley and Duke had been known to set the cat quite literally among the pigeons in some of their more memorable ventures.

The journey from Kensington to Cumbria would be a long one, but she hoped that she and Duke might befriend some other passengers over the hours. She still received postcards from that young man, Hugh, she had met on the train to Exeter that summer. Nice young man, although his interest in taxidermy made Duke bridle somewhat.

She wondered what Mr Howton had had in mind when he had invited her to his supposedly haunted hotel.

She supposed that he had read that rather overblown feature about her in *Spiritualism Now*. Fancied himself the one to change her mind about all this bunkum. The one who could convert Mrs Amelia Thewley, famed sceptic, uncompromising naysayer, into a simpering wreck with a few clanking pipes and a couple of bejewelled spirit-conjurors. Mrs Thewley could hold nothing against the man: by all accounts (and Mrs Thewley had heard Mr Howton's name mentioned more than once in the circles in which she moved), he was said to be a harmless creature, desperately attempting to vault on to the bandwagon of Spiritualism in order to cobble together a few pounds.

Duke jumped up on to the counterpane of her bed, which Mrs Thewley proceeded to straighten. Twenty years ago, she had bought this. Quality never aged, that was her motto. One of her mottos, at least.

The invitation was on her bedside table. She had found the wax seal hugely amusing: to give credit where credit was due, Mr Howton's use of bats was certainly appealing directly to the audience of spectrally inclined visitors that he hoped to lure up to Cumbria.

Dear Mrs Thewley,
You are hereby invited to attend the grand opening
of Maybridge Castle. Séances, Tarot readings and

*ghosts await. You will find your life and your
thoughts upon the great hereafter changed for
ever – 15 December to 18 December 1936.*
    Please RSVP at your earliest convenience.
    Yours,
    Charles Howton

*P.S. Needless to say, the doors of Maybridge Castle
will be very pleased to also welcome your
companion Duke.*

Concise and to the point. She admired that. Oddly
unadorned writing style, but so be it. Mr Howton was,
she imagined, conserving all of his creativity for the
staged shenanigans and rehearsed visitations that were
to occur during the three-night stay.

Duke had settled into sleep by now, relaxing in what
Mrs Thewley referred to as his croissant pose: neatly
curled into a crescent shape resembling those delicious
pastries she and Arthur had so enjoyed in between their
more colourful Montmartre wanderings all those years
ago.

Mrs Thewley stroked Duke's ears absent-mindedly.
The beginnings of something were making themselves
known. She had had a light breakfast – a simple porridge
with a nettle tea – so it couldn't be one of her funny

turns. No, there was something else. Something that was starting to tickle that corner of her brain that usually fluttered into action when she found herself up against a charlatan clairvoyant or a fraudulent medium. She looked again at the invitation.

Maybridge Castle. It was Maybridge Castle that was behind it. Only a few hours now until she would be there. Until Mrs Thewley would uncover quite what it was about Maybridge Castle that was unsettling her.

2

Daphne woke with a start, her head thumping inelegantly against the train's window. Her mouth was dry, and as she rubbed her eyes she made a brief checklist of matters to be addressed. To be brushed off her skirt: a surprising abundance of crumbs from the ham sandwich she had devoured some two hours ago. To be cracked: three final clues in today's cryptic crossword. To be ignored: the couple in the seats across the aisle from her who had been bickering since the journey began at Euston station.

'I keep telling you, I don't know her from Adam,' came a hissed whisper from the man. 'Thursday I was down the Crooked Billet with Frank; that whippet of his came in like the clappers, won us all a nice little bundle.'

Daphne rolled her eyes and sighed and glanced at her wristwatch. The squabble had not changed tenor in the three and a half hours she had been confined to this carriage.

While the woman mounted a riposte in aggressively hushed tones, Daphne shifted in her seat and rubbed a porthole in the misted veil of the window. She knew she ought to sit in soothed awe at the great expanses of the English countryside rolling out around her, and wonder at the green and pleasant land that was enveloping her as the train juddered its way closer to its destination, the Lake District. However, December drizzle had rendered the green and pleasant land rather grey and soggy.

Besides which, she was missing London already.

This solo visit to Cumbria was not, Daphne had rue-fully emphasised in the days leading up to it, how she would prefer to be spending a weekend – three entire nights – away from her desk in December. She fished the invitation out of her satchel. Charles. Charles Howton. Black sheep of Veronica's family, famed for his devil-may-care approach to entrepreneurial endeavours and lackadaisical (or inept, if one were being ungenerous) eye for finances, Cousin Charles had some months ago ploughed what remained of his fortune into Maybridge Castle. Once a crumbling relic of Cumbrian grandeur, it was now . . . a crumbling relic of Cumbrian grandeur pos-ited by its new owner as England's first ever haunted hotel.

And Daphne was spending three nights there, alone, thanks to the 'Broadway shenanigans' mentioned in Charles's invitation.

Addressed to 'Darling cousin Veronica and dear old Daphne', the missive had undoubtedly been crafted to appeal to Daphne's sensationalist side.

Maybridge Castle summons you for a sojourn with the spirits – and your doting cousin, Charles. Why don't the pair of you join me for our grand opening? There'll be Tarot readings from the famous Madame Marla, séances with the dearly departed, crystal balls and all manner of spectacle to inspire you both.

Veronica, you can have a break from all your Broadway shenanigans. Daphne, you can leave your typewriter and your magnifying glass behind, enjoy some respite from uncovering criminal conspiracies and throwing the book at crooks.

Do say you'll come!

Love,

Charles

'Crikey, he's really hamming it up for us, isn't he, V?' Daphne drawled, wincingly sipping the extremely potent coffee that Veronica insisted on serving.

'He never was one to hold back, dear Cousin Charles,' Veronica called from the bathroom. 'Heavens knows who else he'll be inviting. A merry band of chumps and wannabes desperate to ... commuuuuune with the spiiiiiirits.'

'Well, one never knows, Veronica,' Daphne rejoined, swallowing another mouthful of the bitter coffee. 'Cousin Charles might be the one to have broached that heretofore unimpeachable division between the living and the dead. We might be bumping into all sorts of apparitions.'

'Oh quite. I heard that Marie Antoinette booked herself a little weekend there in December: perhaps our dates will coincide?' Veronica emerged from the bathroom, tightening her dressing gown. 'Now that you mention it, Charles did say he had a reservation under the name Ripper, Jack the. Daphne King might finally bring that nasty brute to justice.'

Veronica's digs were rewarded with a grin from Daphne. 'I shall be cracking no cases, following precisely zero clues, refusing to sniff out any rascals whatsover. You do keep telling me I need little respite from my ... calling.'

'Quite, darling,' Veronica agreed as she poured herself a coffee from the ornate silver pot and sat with her legs draped across the arm-rest of the dark green sofa. 'Just think of all the jolly hearty hiking we'll do up there in the wilds of Cumbria. No crimes for you, no pretentious theatre parties for me ... just fresh air, ghosts, and a rum lot of "special guests" gathered by dear Cousin Charles.'

Daphne looked up. 'Not quite sure which of those scares me most.'

'Oh the guests, Daphne: always the guests.'

Thinking back to that morning, Daphne retrieved a bar of Fry's chocolate cream from her bag, and, unwrapping it, reflected once more on her situation. Yes, of course she was delighted – thrilled – that Veronica's play was doing so well in its New York incarnation. So well that Veronica was required to visit the theatre once again to, as she had put it, 'Feather the nest and press the flesh.'

Daphne bit off a chunk of the chocolate.

For yes, Daphne knew that life as a playwright was a precarious one, and Lord knew that Veronica had paid her dues and earned the right to have her name upon a New York billboard.

Another chunk of the chocolate.

And yes, of course Daphne knew that she herself ought to indulge in a break away from the grim business of reporting on the unsavoury dealings of London's law-breakers and malefactors. It had been a taxing few months – taxing though thrilling. What with the Lord Marcus investigation (Daphne had smelled a rat from the word go) and that brute Weeple throwing his weight around the East End, Daphne had been spinning rather a lot of plates. Yes, all in all, Daphne ought to go and regale Cousin Charles with her tales of crime-busting, take in some of that countryside air and pretend to believe in ghosts.

All while Veronica sauntered around the Big Apple, cooking up her next play and air-kissing the great and the good of Broadway. And air-kissing had better be the end of it, Daphne thought, reaching for another chunk of chocolate, only to discover that the bar had vanished during her ruminations.

Nothing like a Fry's Chocolate Cream to take the edge off one's bitterness. In any case, Veronica would be back from New York in a fortnight, in time for a Christmas spent in London. Which reminded Daphne: she must see about that scarf from Liberty's, the one that Veronica had been coveting and dropping hints about since the winter season had begun.

Daphne's reverie was interrupted by the hiss and sputter of the train as it slowed to a stop at Asperdale. Hastily, Daphne retrieved her belongings from the luggage rack, and stuffed her newspaper and notebook into her satchel.

The woman across from her was now sobbing, her eyes fixed dolefully on the man.

'I'm – sorry – John,' she stuttered in between whimpers. 'I know I must stop accusing you, it's all my own fault . . .'

The aforesaid John had his arms folded, an expression of satisfaction on his face.

'Too right it's your own fault, Jenny,' he said, the curl of a smile appearing. 'We just need to calm down, don't we?'

Daphne inhaled deeply. Of course, it didn't do to meddle. No, one should never meddle where one wasn't wanted. But if one happened to share an observation that might assist certain parties. Well, that was quite different.

'Jenny, is it?' she asked as she began to make her way to the carriage exit.

The woman nodded meekly, while the man frowned at this unwelcome interruption.

'Jenny,' Daphne continued, 'do excuse me, but if I were you, I might dry my eyes and ask – John, is it? – I might ask John how it was that he could have been at the Crooked Billet last Thursday when it was closed. Terrible to-do with the lavatories, so I understand. Reopened on Monday, as it happens.'

The woman dabbed her face with her handkerchief, turning to look at the dumbstruck man beside her.

'Now you look here, Miss . . . ?' he began, unfolding his arms and pointing an accusing finger at Daphne.

'King.'

'Miss King, I don't know who you think you are, sticking your beak into other people's business. What are you, a professional nosy parker?' The man rose from his seat for this rather weak jab.

'Oh, much worse,' Daphne replied. 'I'm a retired advice columnist and a full-time investigative reporter. And a little advice for you: if you're going to lie, at least make a convincing show of it.'

And with that, Daphne stepped out on to the Asperdale train platform.

Cousin Charles had arranged for 'his man' to collect Daphne at the train station, despite her protestations that really she would prefer the walk. Cousin Charles had very sensibly pointed out that, firstly, the five-mile walk through the cold, icy lanes would take Daphne well over an hour – even if she were striding at her habitual formidable pace. Secondly, as Charles had so eloquently put it: she hadn't the foggiest where she was going. At this, Daphne had harrumphed, but acquiesced. She hadn't met the man before but spotted a likely candidate instantly: dressed in a black suit and bearing an expression of solemnity, he carried with him the air of a particularly dour undertaker. Daphne would have been only slightly surprised were he to lead her to a hearse.

'Awfully nice of you to collect me, Mr Moore,' Daphne said, her breath appearing as fog while she spoke. 'Last of the guests to arrive, so I gather?'

Moore, unsmiling and taciturn, gave a nod.

'Charles told me on the telephone yesterday that it's a rather eclectic crowd. I believe "ripe for larks" were his words,' Daphne continued, striding alongside Mr Moore, who seemed intent on ignoring her as one might a buzzing fly. As responses to her conversational sallies went, this was a fairly mild one. So far in her year-long career as investigative reporter for the *Chronicle*, Daphne had met with far worse than stony silence.

Daphne found herself continuing to witter inanely as Mr Moore dutifully conveyed her to his automobile. Mercifully, the drive to the castle lasted only around ten minutes. During which time, Mr Moore answered her questions in a manner that brought the phrase 'blood out of stone' thuddingly to mind. Daphne occupied herself by peering at the solemn stone church (was that the one dating back to 1189? Yes, Miss King, Moore confirmed), the seemingly silent flocks of sheep dotting the narrow road (Herdwicks, were they? Yes, Miss King, Moore verified).

Maybridge Castle lay at the end of a winding driveway lined by a row of ill-disciplined trees. To the right, the woodland that was home to a small chapel and a graveyard – in the dimming late afternoon light, Daphne could just make out some scattered headstones. To the left, a vast paddock ruled by, as Daphne would discover, three unruly pigs with a strong possessive streak.

As Mr Moore closed the car door behind her, Daphne glanced up at the castle. It looked every bit the relic that it was. Moss lay undisturbed between the flagstones in front of its large wooden door. Daphne, whose erstwhile life as an advice columnist had lent her a tremendous insight into all varieties of domestic life, spotted a leaky gutter pipe and made a note to alert Charles to it – though she doubted that such a mundane detail would feature highly in his priorities. Despite the castle's evident state of wear, two incongruously extravagant Christmas trees had been positioned on either side of its slightly warped wooden door. Baubles swayed in the cold breeze, frost glittered on the branches. Atop each tree was a figure. Daphne stood on tiptoes to examine each one: not angels, but small woollen bats wearing red hats. A pleasingly macabre touch. Standing back again, she looked up at the building. She found the castle oddly mesmerising. Not precisely charming, for that implied a warmth, a desire to make others feel at ease. As Daphne continued to assess its exterior – the higgledy-piggledy patchwork of bricks clearly from various eras throughout its long life, the boarded up window somewhere on the top floor, the swallows' nests lining one side of the roof – she had the odd impression of the castle reciprocating the scrutiny. That it was peering at her and evaluating her worth as a guest. As the thought struck her, a chill crept down her spine.

'Blimey,' Daphne muttered to herself wryly as Mr Moore opened the front door for her. 'Not even crossed the threshold and already I'm imagining myself a damsel from a Gothic novel. Must be all those hooded monks and diabolical spirits.'

It would be but a few hours, however, before Daphne realised that ghostly apparitions were the least of the dangers to be found in Maybridge Castle.

3

Daphne wavered at the threshold. The air had a dry, tart snap. A saltiness that tautened her senses. Mr Moore noticed her hesitation.

'The matter?' he grunted.

Daphne's perplexed expression prompted him to elaborate.

'That is to say, is there anything the matter . . . ma'am?' Mr Moore said, shifting her case from one hand to the other.

'Not at all, Mr Moore,' Daphne replied. It was three o'clock. Dusk would be falling soon. Daphne felt a prickling within her. A restlessness that fizzed and jangled. Her breath formed a mist before her, and she pressed into the frost beneath her with her shoes. She couldn't quite bring herself to go indoors just yet. It had been a stultifying train journey, and now she felt an urgent need to awaken herself. To get the measure of this place which seemed to be getting the measure of her.

'Mr Moore, would you mind awfully if you were to bring my suitcase to my room while I ... explore?' She gestured to the grounds around her. 'I find my new location rather irresistible. I fear I damn near contracted permanent pins and needles on that train; roaming's the only remedy I know for such an ailment.'

Daphne presented Mr Moore with her most guileless smile. She was rewarded with a frown.

'I'll be in in a jiffy, but of course if dearest Charles wishes to gift me with a welcome embrace ... he can always come and find me! Toodle-pip!' Daphne spun away from the heavy door, creaking with warped wood, before Mr Moore could articulate any objection.

The gravel drive to the castle was a winding one that, from her vantage point atop a slight hill, sliced between the woodlands and the paddock. Daphne took a few crunching steps away from the main building and its prying windows. Opposite the castle was what looked to be a tumbledown stable. Several strides towards it, avoiding a rather perilous-looking frozen puddle, and the odour of rotting hay confirmed this hypothesis. Daphne peered into the stable, and, in the dimming light, could see only an assortment of stacked crates and various nondescript structures draped in moth-eaten and stained sheets.

Charles really would need to take some action about this eyesore, she thought. It wouldn't do for his guests to be welcomed by the distinct sweet aroma of hay that was past its best.

A sudden beating of wings startled Daphne and she turned towards the paddock. A collection of rowdy crows had just taken flight, seemingly being chased by an alarmingly swift, heavyset pig. She could hear the comical 'oinks' as the creature galloped after the birds. Daphne's eyebrows rose in surprise: here she was thinking that pigs were content trotting from one bowl of slop to another and rolling in excrement. Judging by this beast's temperament and movement, the pigs of Cumbria were rather more partial to tearing through fields and signalling their dominance through a series of raucous snorts.

Daphne pulled her gloves from her pockets: the temperature was decidedly frostier here than in London, but the sky above was clearer, the dimming light still more piercing and of a purer texture than the dreary sky which had hung above the city when she had left that morning.

Standing at the edge of the field, amusing herself by listening to – and attempting to interpret – the grunts of the pig and its two companions who had emerged from a trough further down the paddock, Daphne inhaled deeply. There was salt in the air. Charles had mentioned that there was a small beach nearby, one which looked across the Solway, and from where, on a particularly clear day, one could see Scotland. There was a stillness that subdued her jangling restlessness. Perhaps the country wasn't as bad as all that, after all. Where in the metropolis could one find such repose for one's mind? Certainly not on Fleet Street.

She took a few strides around the side of the stable, away from the castle. Ah, here it was: Maybridge Castle's famous maze.

Involuntarily, Daphne murmured, 'My, my.'

The fading grandeur of the maze was evident, even in the wintry, cold light. She felt herself drawn towards it, and, approaching, she could see black creatures darting hither and thither in the sky above it. Their movements appeared erratic, unpredictable at first. Then Daphne realised that there was a scattered synchronicity to their sudden flickering. Bats. The inspiration behind Charles's seal, no doubt. Momentarily mesmerised, Daphne watched as they hastened in loops above the maze.

The maze itself was a forbidding sight. Although stripped of leaves now, the hedges still loomed impressively high – at least six feet tall, Daphne estimated. Frost twinkled upon the bare branches, an oddly festive juxtaposition with the desolate hedges and the darkness that seemed to swallow up the two pathways leading into the centre of the maze.

An adventure for another day, Daphne thought as she

pulled her coat tighter and jammed her hands into her pockets. Rampaging pigs, skittering bats, a dilapidated stable and a forbidding maze. So far, Charles's descriptions of Maybridge Castle and its environs were aligning precisely: Cousin Charles had always, according to Veronica, been prone to exaggeration, embellishments, but not even he, Daphne suspected, could outdo Maybridge's own theatrical flourishes. Now all she needed to inspect was the aviary: supposedly dating back to that grand period of Victorian self-aggrandisement, the aviary had once been home to various species of parrots that had been transported from far more exotic climes. The poor creatures had, of course, perished when whisked to the inhospitable temperatures of Cumbria. Daphne glanced at her watch. Nearly half past three. Although she was tempted to sally forth and investigate the aviary, two factors prompted hesitation: Charles had stressed that the aviary was strictly out of bounds (something to do with some nesting wrens, Daphne seemed to recall), and the fact that her stomach had begun to rumble. That ham sandwich on the train hadn't quite sated her.

As if in answer to her prevarication, Daphne heard a trilling voice calling her name.

'Daphneeee! Halloooooooo!'

Cousin Charles. His voice was coming from the

direction of the castle. His man Moore must have alerted him to Daphne's arrival and subsequent wanderings.

'Come out, come out wherever you are!' Charles called again.

Gone were the tranquillity and the repose. Evidently, it was now the hour for Daphne to emerge from solitude into sociability.

'Daaaaaaphne!'

She glimpsed back at the maze and the shadowy aviary. Tomorrow, she thought. Tomorrow she would see what else Maybridge Castle was hiding up its sleeve.

4

Cousin Charles was leaning on his cane outside the front door to the castle. He waved effusively when he saw Daphne striding towards him.

'Ah, there you are, darling D,' he beamed, stretching out one arm to pull her into an embrace. 'How dare you take yourself off gallivanting, Daphne! Don't you know that I've a whole tour designed for that sort of thing? Anecdotes abounding about woebegone maidens plagued by unearthly beings, disembodied Tudor barons lurking around every corner. And so on and so forth.'

Daphne grinned. Ever the showman, since purchasing Maybridge Castle, Charles had been positively fizzing with excitement about his tales – fabricated in the last six months, no doubt – of historical ghouls and uncanny apparitions. And, in venturing forth alone, Daphne had robbed him of the opportunity to establish the grounds as a hotbed of phantasmagorical happenings.

'Oh don't worry, Charles,' she responded. 'I've yet to set foot inside: you can treat me to a thorough rundown of all the demons, banshees and revenants that await me.'

'Now, now, Daphne,' Charles replied with a smile. 'I'll none of your cynicism. Maybridge Castle is host to the most exclusive phantoms in the land. No common or garden ghouls, I'll thank you to acknowledge.'

Despite his mischievous demeanour, Charles had aged since Daphne had last seen him. There was a weariness around his eyes, his smile more forced than it ought to be. He hugged his coat about him, as if the cold were rattling his bones, and he seemed to be leaning more heavily than usual on his ornate cane.

She was about to enquire after the arrangements for her stay and the other guests who would be joining her, when she was interrupted by the jovial tooting of a car horn.

'Oh! Another of our special guests! My dear old friend Raymond Hammond!' Charles exclaimed, turning his attention to the car that had wended its away along the drive. Daphne watched Charles as he squinted at the car. Did his smile falter, the closer the car came? Was that a fleeting glimpse of disappointment flickering across his face?

'Ah . . .' Charles murmured.

'What is it?' Daphne asked, craning her head to the car.

'Oh . . . nothing, nothing. Just . . . Raymond's brought his son, Kenneth,' came Charles's reply. 'Bit of a . . . handful, that's all. But I'm sure it's nothing that Maybridge Castle can't manage!'

The car pulled up slowly outside the stable and two men stepped out. The older, Raymond, looked roughly fifty, Charles's contemporary. Where Charles still boasted an impressively luxurious head of greying hair, Raymond was bald. His paunch, red cheeks and benevolent smile called to mind the Santa Claus that Daphne had seen ringing a bell on Fleet Street yesterday evening. The older man's apparent jollity was, however, offset by his son's glowering demeanour. His face would have been handsome, Daphne reflected, were it not for its pinched expression. Rangy and lean, the younger man was dressed only in a shirt and trousers, no sensible layers to affront the winter. The folly of youth, Daphne thought, judging him to be around twenty.

'Charles!' the older man said. 'What a pleasure – as always – to see you! And what a pile you've nabbed here, eh?' He gestured towards the castle.

Daphne watched as Charles hobbled towards his new guest and extended an arm towards him. Raymond clapped an arm around Charles and they walked towards the boot of the car.

'Delighted you could make it, Raymond. I so hoped that you would; truly I did,' Charles said. He turned to the younger man, who was holding himself in aloof provocation on the passenger side of the car. Charles's voice took on a more formal, distant tone. 'Kenneth. Welcome.'

Kenneth pursed his lips, as if considering his response. His face became momentarily animated, as if he was readying himself for an outburst. At the very instant at which Daphne was sure he was about to launch into a reply, his father patted his arm gently. The young man tensed. Sighed in resignation or frustration.

He held out his hand and stiffly shook Charles's, uttering a barely audible, 'Yes, here we are. As instructed – I mean, invited.'

Just as her nerves had jangled earlier, Daphne felt a tingling sensation. It was a sensation she often felt when encountering something that was ... amiss. Veronica had likened it to the tautened senses of a bloodhound just as the hunt was beginning. Charles and Kenneth, some lingering enmity there. Something to be pursued. She stopped herself. Must she suspect every Tom, Dick and Harry of harbouring some hideous secret? Must she dislodge every stone in her path and examine the worms writhing beneath it? It was a rather exhausting habit, she had come to find. But a deliciously exhausting one.

'Come, come.' Charles ushered them all towards the castle. 'Out of this perishing cold. Leave your bags – my man Moore will collect them for you. In we go: Maybridge Castle and all its unearthly delights lie in wait!'

5

Stepping into Maybridge Castle, Daphne was struck by a heady concoction of smells: a damp mustiness that told of centuries of cold winters; a seasonal mixture of fir tree, cloves and oranges; a tantalising whiff of, yes, roast lamb. Charles shrugged off his coat and hung it upon a stand just inside the door. Daphne wasn't ready to give hers up just yet, the chill of the outdoors still clinging to her.

'How about a little tour of the ground floor?' Charles suggested, a twinkle in his eye.

A sidelong glance at Kenneth Hammond told Daphne that the young man would not be accepting the invitation willingly. Evidently, his father had surmised as much and replied graciously on his son's behalf.

'Oh, I think Kenneth and I are rather exhausted after that drive. Norwich to Cumbria does take its toll on one,' Raymond explained, patting his son on the shoulder. 'Perhaps your man Moore can show us to our rooms?'

'Of course, of course, you must be in need of a rest, Raymond,' Charles answered, a hint of disappointment in his voice. 'Although I'm afraid it's just the one room between you. On the first floor, only the front half of the building gets any heat, which has rendered five of the bedrooms utterly uninhabitable. Hoping to have them up and running by, say, this time next year.'

Charles chuckled, though Daphne failed to see exactly what the joke was. It was something of a concern if half of the bedrooms in England's most haunted hotel were unable to be occupied by paying guests. Daphne made an inward note to relay this to Veronica. Diplomatically, of course. Charles's finances were a source of perpetual vexation for his family, and his new venture operating at only 50 per cent capacity – at a maximum – would raise eyebrows at best. And cause a family fracas at worst.

The front door was flung open and Mr Moore's hulking frame appeared; he was carrying the suitcases that the Hammond men had left in their car. Charles instructed him to show the father and son to the twin room that they were to share.

Turning to Daphne, Charles grinned and said, 'Right-o, dearest D. Let's show you what's what here at Maybridge Castle.'

The entrance hallway was a rather bare welcome to the castle. Aside from the coat-stand, the only other piece of furniture was a small brown table upon which was a framed article from the *Asperdale Gazette* dated 31 October 1909. Daphne peered at it and read: 'Maybridge Castle killings – family slain in mystery attack.'

'I knew you'd be straight to that, Daphne,' Charles said with a wag of his finger. 'Nasty business, of course: entire family, whole lot of them, murdered. Never caught the brute who did it – though folks around here say it was the stable hand, possessed by the devil.'

Daphne was sceptical. 'Are you quite sure you didn't just run this through your typewriter last month, Charles?'

The walls of the hallway were flaking cream-coloured paint (soon to be replaced with a crimson red, Charles assured her), and a patch of mould was growing from the skirting board in one very unfortunately prominent spot (a lad from the village was going to see to that, Charles explained).

The first room off the hallway to the right revealed itself to be the drawing room. Daphne poked her head around the door and was astounded by the contrast with the barren hallway that had ushered her into the castle. The drawing room resembled the private collection of a Victorian gentleman. Trinkets and *objets* were crammed into every nook and cranny, while impressively sturdy mahogany shelves decked each wall.

Daphne gazed at the taxidermised stoat that skulked

upon a shelf in one corner, next to a bronzed diving helmet that could well have been snatched directly from the pages of *Twenty Thousand Leagues Under the Sea*. Daphne found herself walking into the room as if in a trance. The Natural History Museum was but a cheap pier gift shop compared to this trove. She picked up a large conch and then set it back down beside a sculpture of a stag. A fat black candle was in an elaborate wrought-iron candlestick, hardened wax dripping down it. Two shelves were dedicated to dusty old hardbacks, titles of which ran the gamut from *Occultist Phenomena: or How to Reach Beyond the Great Divide* to *Wonderful Preserves*.

In the centre of the room were two plush sofas and an armchair. The fire in the hearth was already roaring, and on the mantelpiece above it Daphne could see various Christmas cards that had already arrived for Charles.

She turned to look at him, and returned his smile of contentment.

'Charles, this is . . .'

'Wonderful, isn't it?' he replied. 'As you'll see, I've had to be rather, shall we say, selective, about which rooms to invest in. As the drawing room, it was only right that this should be furnished in such a way as to—'

'Be bloody impressive?' Daphne completed his sentence. 'It feels – well, so *right*, Charles. So *complete*. So . . . *proper*.'

'I shan't take your surprise personally, Daphne,' Charles said, approaching the small drinks trolley in the corner. 'I do have some acumen and flair, dontcha know.'

He poured a ginger wine for her. 'A little refreshment for the rest of the tour. And fear not: you'll have ample time to delve into these shelves when we meet for pre-dinner drinks here later.'

Upon exiting the drawing room, Daphne was met anew with the cold sterility of the entrance hallway. She followed Charles along the corridor, her eyes cast down at the threadbare green carpet underfoot; she tried to avoid glancing too often at the smatterings of mould which were the corridor's only decorations. Charles was wittering amiably about the roast lamb that was to be their dinner that night and the 'crumpets of unparalleled deliciousness' that would await them at breakfast the next morning.

'She's a wonder, our Mrs Moore,' Daphne heard him say. 'A rival to Mrs Beeton, I should say.'

The corridor opened out on a small tiled area, an odd space that Charles had evidently decided should be home to a startling suit of armour. A black, multi-pronged candlestick of about waist height was beside the armour, and it had been festooned with holly sprigs. Atop the knight's head was a Father Christmas hat that lent the scene a surreal dimension. Behind the knight was a large window, through which Daphne could see the paddock. The sky was tinged with pink, and, although it was not yet four o'clock, the North Star was already visible.

'Do bid Sir Otranto a good afternoon, won't you Daphne,' Charles said as he tipped his head towards the knight. 'Awfully bad luck to ignore him. Lord knows what fire and brimstone might rain down upon us should you fail to demonstrate adequate courtliness.'

The aroma of roast lamb was growing stronger, and, having made obeisance to Sir Otranto, Daphne followed Charles to the next room. Inside was the dining room, a more formal setting than the drawing room. An imposing dining table was situated in the middle of the room. Set around it were ten tall chairs which, Daphne reflected, looked as though they had been plucked directly from a medieval torture chamber.

On the wall above the table was a portrait that immediately provoked a powerful unease in Daphne that she couldn't place. A man and a woman stood rigidly side by side. Their attire suggested the eighteenth century: frock coats, elaborate hairpieces. A greyhound was perched by their side. Their eyes possessed a cavernous depth that also seemed hollow, as if both were suppressing immense despair. Looking closer, she saw that the female figure's left hand was clenched into a fist beside her lavender dress.

'Fetching couple, eh?' Charles joked. 'The very image of marital bliss. Lord and Lady Holmcroft. Ruled the roost here at Maybridge Castle for, oooh, best part of fifty years.'

Daphne looked closer and saw that, yes, behind the pair was Maybridge Castle.

'What happened to them?' she asked. For something within her told her that something *had* happened to them. She took a sip of her ginger wine.

'Ah, now that's quite the story,' Charles replied gleefully, even giddily. 'Lady Holmwood's great-aunt lived to a ripe old age of one hundred and nine, all told. They had her up in the attic – naturally. In fact, look a little closer, won't you, D?'

On tiptoe, Daphne examined the painting further. There, up in the top-left corner of the painting: a window at the top of Maybridge Castle. An elderly woman was glaring out of it. Although only perhaps an inch of the painting, now that Daphne had spotted her, the figure dominated the work.

'Lummy,' Daphne murmured. 'So the great-aunt . . . ?'

'Butcher's knife in the night,' Charles mimed slicing his throat. 'Both of 'em, done in.'

'Of course, both of 'em, done in,' Daphne echoed. 'What else would one expect of Maybridge Castle and its colourful history?'

'Speaking of butcher's knives – let's to the kitchen, shall we? Simply *dying* for you to meet Mrs Moore.'

With that, Charles spirited Daphne back out into the corridor. They strolled past two more doors (rooms regrettably out of service: heck of a case of black rot in both, Charles confided), and to a door at the very end of the hallway. As he flung it open, the smell of roast lamb erupted from within. Daphne's stomach gurgled.

The kitchen was perhaps twice the size of the drawing room. Cupboards lined the two walls either side of the door, while the wall opposite was filled with small windows that looked out on to the woodland. The surfaces were laden with all manner of treats: a plate of mince pies; some cold cuts and cheese; a pie decorated intricately with perfectly golden pastry.

A woman stooped over the large rustic table in the middle. Plainly dressed in black, she was humming gently.

'Allow me to introduce the marvellous Mrs Moore: queen of all you see before you!' Charles bowed deeply, and his proclamation had prompted Mrs Moore to drop her spatula.

'Begging your pardon, sir,' she replied meekly, nodding her head and fixing her eyes on an indistinct spot on the kitchen flagstones. She began to wipe her hands on her apron.

'No pardon to be begged, Mrs Moore, I simply

wanted our latest arrival, Miss Daphne King, to experience the wonders of your domain,' Charles said as he sidled towards the plate of mince pies and deftly pocketed one. 'We shall await your roast lamb dinner with salivating mouths and gaping stomachs.'

With that visceral image dispensed, Charles suggested that Daphne head to her room, while he waited to greet the remaining arrivals.

As they ambled along the corridor, Daphne could hear Mrs Moore recommence her humming back in the kitchen. Charles was burbling again (his giddiness really knew no bounds), as a staccato sneeze echoed along the corridor, emanating from one of the sealed-off, black rot rooms.

'One of the village lads, attending to the black rot? Jolly well hope it doesn't creep into the poor boy's lungs,' Daphne commented blithely.

Charles paused. 'Nobody in those rooms, far as I know. Must be one of our dearly departed spirits, allergic to Christmas trees or some shimsham like that.'

6

While Daphne situated herself in the room that was to be hers for the next three nights, Charles Howton was showing another guest to her room. A guest who would come to play a vital role in Daphne's stay.

'Of course, there have always been ghosts here at Maybridge Castle,' Charles Howton explained cheerily, grasping a cane in one hand and in the other the wicker basket he had insisted on carrying for his guest. 'Misunderstood souls, wandering spirits. Madame Marla conversed with a chap just the other week who'd died by cannon fire during the Civil War. Wanted her to pass on a rather . . . ripe message to Oliver Cromwell.'

He paused and turned around, lowering his voice confidentially. 'You can imagine the furore when Madame Marla told him he was several centuries too late for that. Shuddering windows, creaking floorboards, clanking pipes. Poor fellow's calmed down since then, thank goodness.'

Mrs Amelia Thewley smiled serenely, steadying herself against the wall. 'Quite the disappointment, one imagines. Now, Mr Howton, I must confess that my spry demeanour belies my decrepitude: I did, after all, celebrate my seventy-fifth birthday just last week. That being the case, I do rather fear that I might be in danger of expiring and joining your legions of spectres if I'm forced to climb another staircase . . .'

Charles beamed at her and gave an extravagant bow, gesturing towards a burgundy door and producing a dramatically oversized copper key from his pocket. 'Make yourself at home, Mrs Thewley. My man, Moore, will bring the rest of your cases up shortly. And you'll meet your fellow guests over some pre-dinner drinks – commencing in precisely one hour. And there will, of course, be Christmas carols around the piano for anyone so inclined.'

'Meeting the *living* fellow guests, I assume you mean?' Amelia replied with a chuckle.

Charles winked and unlocked the door with a flourish. 'That I do. As for the other residents of Maybridge Castle: I presume no control over their movements, I'm afraid, but they do tend to be a fairly timid lot at this hour of the day. So I hope that you and your companion shan't be intruded upon – just yet.'

Having bade farewell to her host, Amelia pulled the

door closed behind her and set her basket down on the floor, unfastening it with practised ease. The lid instantly flipped open and out leapt said companion. The tabby purred enthusiastically and sniffed the air with curiosity.

'Here we are, Duke,' she proclaimed. 'Now we must mind our manners this time; no upsetting the apple cart like we did at the last place.'

The apple cart had well and truly been upset during Amelia Thewley's most recent expedition in her self-professed mission to debunk, expose and otherwise unveil proponents of the paranormal as counterfeiters and tricksters. After the episode in Margate, all employees of the spiritual grotto had been ordered to deny entry in perpetuity to a certain shrewd lady of advanced years. Her nephew, Rupert, had, of course, indulged in his habitual eye-rolling and head-shaking, berating Amelia for her 'pig-headed and dogged charging around like a bull in a china shop.' Amelia had gently suggested that Rupert stick with one animal-based idiom per insult, feedback which had prompted unintelligible muttering from her one remaining relative.

Straightening herself up and unbuttoning her cardigan, Amelia glanced about the room. One had to admit that Charles Howton had done a rather splendid job of it. Despite the rather unprepossessing exterior, once inside no detail had been overlooked in the new hotelier's quest to transform Maybridge Castle into an opulent den of Spiritualism. A four-poster bed stood imposingly in the centre of the room, surrounded by all manner of paraphernalia. Here, a rather forceful print asking 'DO SPIRITS RETURN?', there a stack of dusty volumes of M. R. James. And was that, in the corner . . . ? No, it couldn't be. Amelia frowned and approached a small mahogany table, upon which sat an inert black taxidermised cat. It glared malignly at Amelia, as well you might, she reasoned, if you had been stuffed and left on a table in the Cumbrian countryside. She swiftly – and, of course, respectfully – covered the specimen with a spare doily, lest Duke set eyes upon his fallen kin. Throughout the room, the solitary concession to the festive season was a somewhat macabre-looking arrangement of holly in a black vase. Amelia approved, not being one for tinsel and trifles.

Yes, she thought, this would do nicely. She lowered herself slowly into a plush red armchair and sighed. The journey up from London had been something of a trial, passengers bullishly squabbling over space for all the parcels and packages that were destined to sit underneath their Christmas trees for three more weeks. Duke had been as well behaved as usual, uttering but one meow in the six hours that the train had taken to trundle its way to the village of Asperdale. Rupert had, of course, been practically apoplectic when Amelia had informed her nephew of her intention to spend a few days, in his words, 'rattling around a damp pile of bricks'. Whereupon he had launched into an informative and impassioned monologue about the dangers of dry rot. Amelia often marvelled at the one mystery that had so far evaded her powers of logic and explanation: how her dearly departed sister Susan had brought forth such a fussily solicitous stick-in-the-mud as Rupert.

As arranged with Charles Howton, Amelia had been greeted (although that choice of verb did overstate things slightly) at the station by 'his man' Moore. And now, here she sat, in what Charles Howton had proudly declared to be England's first and only bona fide haunted hotel.

Amelia set about installing herself comfortably in her suite. Soon, upon the bedside table sat her cod liver oil, borage ointment and calendula balm. She had cleared some of the more questionably colourful tomes – *those* need not occupy such a prominent position on the bookshelf, she reasoned – to make way for the collection of art that accompanied her and Duke on their travels. Rupert never tired of declaring that it was unseemly for a woman of her age to cart around a hoard of nudes daubed on canvases. Amelia, for her part, merely shrugged off Rupert's prudery and reminded him what a jolly nice time she'd had painting them at the evening class in Chelsea.

'Now, what do we think of Maybridge Castle, Duke?' Amelia tsked and Duke instantly jumped upon her tartan skirt, settling himself down comfortably. 'Shall we see what Mr Howton has up his sleeve? He seems a nice sort. I suspect he might even believe in all this hokum – let's go gently on him and his phantasms, shall we?'

7

Just a few doors along the corridor, Daphne King was also installing herself in her suite. Such an endeavour took approximately four minutes and thirty seconds, given that Daphne's trousseau – such as it was – consisted of the bare essentials: three blouses, one pair of corduroy trousers (which she had now changed into), one notebook, one pen.

She glanced about, admiring, as Mrs Thewley had done, the attention to detail evident in the room. The selection of reading material was an amusing one, and Daphne began to leaf through one of the more colourful tomes placed on the table: *Ghosts, Hobgoblins and the Haunted House* by P. K. Chestlow. A plate of mince pies was on the dressing table, while a sprig of mistletoe hung above the mirror.

The whispering came as Daphne was engrossed in an explanation of how a certain Sir Henry Rubens had put a stop to the pranks of a belligerent shapeshifter in the eighteenth century. Barely perceptible at first, it increased in intensity and, squinting through her glasses, Daphne could make out a shadow moving frantically beneath her door.

Daphne cautiously approached the door, struggling to make out the words being uttered in such hushed but impassioned tones. The acoustics of a haunted castle left more than a little to be desired.

Straining, Daphne frowned. What was it being repeated? A refrain of increasing vehemence. '*It's impossible, impossible . . . won't get away with this . . .*'

The mutterings were interrupted by a machine-gun sneeze and the footsteps receded swiftly.

Daphne's eyes widened. She had been in Maybridge Castle but thirty minutes and already a morsel of intrigue was being dangled before her.

A door slammed somewhere further along the corridor, and the shadow beneath Daphne's door hastily shuffled away, in the direction of the staircase.

In the long, bewildering days to follow, amidst the curious histories that were to emerge, Daphne King would come to regret her sluggishness in this instant. Why the deuce hadn't she opened the door immediately? What possessed her to embody such uncharacteristic inertia? The long train journey had perhaps, as they say, taken it out of her. In any case, by the time Daphne had come to her senses and twisted the doorknob, the space outside her door was empty.

'You silly fool, Daphne,' she began to mutter. 'Act at leisure, repent with haste—'

Daphne's self-flagellating grumbling was interrupted by an overly loud and laboured salutation.

'*Hallo – dear,*' came the woman's voice, each syllable enunciated to within an inch of its life. '*I – say – do – you – need – any – help?*'

Daphne turned to see a young woman of about twenty-five, her black hair curled and set in the 'bob' style that was de rigueur these days. The woman was approaching another figure in the corridor: an elderly lady, barefoot, an expression of intent concentration upon her face. The younger woman was smiling at the older with a mixture of pity, concern and unwarranted friendliness.

'*My – hubby – is a – doctor,*' the woman continued, edging her way cautiously towards the older woman, as if frightened that a sudden movement might trigger a cardiac episode. '*HE – CAN – HELP YOU!*'

Although the corridor was lit only with flickering candles set upon brass sconces, Daphne could make out the elderly woman's face. She looked very much as though this condescending greeting was decidedly getting her goat up.

'Well, duckie, that's very kind of you,' the older woman replied patiently, smiling serenely, 'but I require no assistance. If I do, I'll be sure to call upon your . . . *hubby*.'

Still unseen by the two parties, Daphne smiled to herself. The white-haired lady was exhibiting admirable forbearance in the face of this patronising interloper. Daphne stepped forward, closing the door to her room behind her.

'Hullo both,' she said warmly. 'I take it we're neighbours?'

The young woman turned and beamed at her. 'Oh, hello, good evening. Yes, room seven. Eleanor Beaumont: Mrs Dr John Eleanor Beaumont.' She held out her hand and shook Daphne's hand with surprising vigour.

'Mrs Amelia Thewley,' the white-haired lady offered, hand aloft in a wave. 'And this,' she said, bending down and lifting her cat with unexpected agility, 'is Duke.'

The cat yawned widely in response.

Daphne strolled towards Mrs Thewley, Duke and Eleanor Beaumont. In her tartan skirt and incongruous bare feet, white hair neatly and unfussily pulled into a small bun, Mrs Thewley smiled at Daphne – not the accommodating smile that she had presented to Eleanor Beaumont a minute or two earlier, but a smile that hinted at interest and intrigue.

'Tell me,' Daphne was saying, 'did either of you hear a commotion out here in the corridor?'

Eleanor Beaumont looked blankly, shaking her head. Mrs Thewley, on the other hand, narrowed her eyes and replied, 'As a matter of fact I did – some rather cryptic mutterings, that's why I'm out here sans slippers. Had a little trouble making it out, my hearing's not quite what it used to be. Added to which, Duke was indulging in one of his snoring episodes.'

Daphne smiled. She sensed that the presence of Mrs Amelia Thewley was going to enhance her enjoyment of the next three days immeasurably.

'Oh, here's my hubby now! Here you are John!' Mrs Eleanor Beaumont gestured towards the man coming along the corridor from the opposite direction. Slightly out of breath, John Beaumont produced a handkerchief from his trouser pocket and wiped his forehead as he approached. Daphne assessed him. Neatly clipped moustache, mildly receding hairline, freshly ironed shirt over a moderate paunch. He would have been a perfectly unremarkable figure, had it not been for the concerning pallor of his skin, the visible beads of sweat about his forehead and the dark circles under his eyes.

A doctor in need of an elixir of some kind, Daphne thought.

Mrs Eleanor Beaumont clasped her husband's hand

tightly, rendering it rather awkward for him to shake Daphne's and Mrs Thewley's.

'How do you do, Dr John Beaumont?' Mrs Thewley said. She glanced down at her slipperless feet. 'Please forgive my state of undress: you can rest assured that I'm not in the habit of roaming barefoot distressing young damsels. Wouldn't blame you if you thought I was one of the famous Maybridge Castle ghouls.'

Eleanor giggled and swung her husband's hand. 'We've been told to expect lots of bumps in the night, you see, so I think we're rather on edge.'

John Beaumont certainly gave the impression of a man discomfited. Biting his lip uneasily, he glanced about as if in anticipation of a spectral interruption.

His wife, on the other hand, was the very picture of content radiance. Rosy-cheeked and smiling, she seemed incapable of perturbation.

'And this, John, is . . . ?' she continued in her role of making corridor introductions.

'Miss Daphne King,' Daphne stated, noting Dr John Beaumont's rather limp and clammy handshake.

Eleanor Beaumont beamed brightly, 'Well I suppose we ought to make our way to these pre-dinner drinks – might we help you downstairs, Miss Thewley?'

'*Mrs* Thewley,' the lady replied impishly. 'I may exude the air of a dotty old maid, but I have, to the shock and incredulity of many, played wife at one point or another in my days.'

A blush rose on Eleanor Beaumont's already well-complexioned face.

'I should be delighted to join you all, momentarily,' Mrs Thewley replied impishly. 'Please allow me one moment, however: one cannot, after all, attend a drinks gathering without one's shoes and one's cat.'

8

With Duke obligingly back in his basket, Mrs Thewley had set off with the Beaumonts and Daphne. Eleanor wittered amiably about her and her husband's wedding: they had, it transpired, tied the knot only that summer, and were now on a belated honeymoon.

'John thinks I'm mad as a box of frogs, traipsing all the way to *the North* of all places to find ghosts when it's nearly *Christmas*,' Eleanor was explaining. 'Don't you, darling – mad as a box of frogs!'

A pause before John replied, 'Frogs, yes, darling, the frogs.' Even in the faint light of the corridor, Daphne could make out the shifting expression on John Beaumont's face. When he looked at his wife – really, truly looked at her – the unsettling fretfulness upon his face dissipated, to be replaced with a strangely melancholic gaze. What was prodding away at Mr Beaumont's troubled mind, Daphne wondered. A meow from Duke's basket disturbed Daphne's ruminations – more of that later, she reassured herself.

After descending the stairs and stopping to admire a coat of arms on the wall, the quartet (or quintet, if one counts feline companions. Which, of course, any sound-minded person would) approached the drawing room.

Duke's basket in her right hand, Mrs Thewley twisted the door knob with her left, and the group was met with a rather mirthless scene within the room.

Four people were arranged in a tableau of malaise. There, standing by the fireplace were Raymond and Kenneth Hammond. In the firelight the younger man looked even more lean-faced than when Daphne had seen him earlier, his eyes glowering and his jaw clenched. He clutched a wine glass in one hand, while his other was balled into a fist. His hair casually tousled, he had put on a loose tweed jacket since she had last seen him, but the top button of his shirt was undone and there was no tie in sight. A student, she thought now. The type she often saw mooning around outside King's College on the Strand, or scribbling notes at the British Library.

Raymond was patting his son's arm placatingly, mur-muring quietly with an attempt at a jovial smile upon his face.

A large Regency sofa sat imposingly to the left, its

plush red cushions almost iridescent in the firelight. A woman was draped upon the sofa, dandling a crystal tumbler. As the light from the flames played upon her striking face, Daphne could see that the woman was wearing an expression of smug self-satisfaction. A smirk danced upon her lips, and her eyes – cool, grey, impersonal – glinted with provocative malice. Her manicured hands, black satin dress and heavy string of pearls indicated a woman of expensive taste. Slightly older than Daphne, the woman appeared to be in her mid-forties.

Presiding over all was their host, Charles Howton. Fussing with the drinks cabinet in the corner, he was humming somewhat frantically.

As if raising an eyebrow at the froideur in the room, a huge Christmas tree peered over all assembled, its tinsel arranging itself into a bemused grin. In the corner, the needle of a gramophone scratched repeatedly at the record that had previously, Daphne presumed, been playing some suitably joyful tunes.

Daphne let out a gasp of amusement when she cast her eyes away from the array of uncomfortable guests and saw the spread that lay upon a large table.

Pinks, oranges, reds – even a green. An assortment of elaborate jellies glinted in the flickering lights of the candles that were dotted about the table. Holly leaves, red berries, tiny sugar-plum mice were arranged around the jellies. Daphne took a step towards the table. In the green jelly, some nuts were suspended, while in the red, there looked to be some cranberries floating. The centre-piece was an impressively structured jelly that was shaped like an angel.

'Crikey, is all of this edible?' Daphne asked, of nobody in particular.

Charles Howton spun around, still leaning on his cane, happiness flooding his face at respite represented by the new arrivals. 'Ah, wonderful, here you all are! And yes, these are some of Mrs Moore's finest work: apparently jellies are all the rage now.'

Daphne strolled over to Charles, kissing him on the cheek.

'Daphne, I see you've already made the acquaintance of your neighbours upstairs, how splendid. Allow me to introduce you to our other residents – but first, drinks!'

Mrs Thewley set Duke's basket down on the floor and scooped the cat up swiftly.

'Quite right too, Charles. I've never been one to let social niceties stand between me and a gin. That's my poison of choice, but I also accept sherry if needs be.'

Mrs Thewley took Duke and sat comfortably on the sofa, prompting the woman lounging there with her crystal tumbler to shuffle away from her slightly and let out a snort.

'How delicious! We already have a suburban kook and her put-upon husband,' the woman purred, nodding towards the Beaumonts. 'A pathetically tear-sodden widower and his terribly serious scholarly son, a comically desperate host on the brink of bankruptcy . . .'

The young man by the fireplace glared with even more intensity than before, while Charles sloshed a very liberal serving of gin into a glass.

'And now of course, *of course*, we have ourselves a magnificently eccentric old woman and her faithful cat! Manna from heaven for my review of this place,' the woman concluded with a rambunctious slap to her thigh, throwing back the last of her drink with clear relish.

Mrs Thewley chuckled. 'A faithful cat, yes, but I demur at the moniker "magnificently eccentric". I fear you'll find me a frightfully banal creature, Miss . . . ?'

'And I fear you'll find *her* frightfully cruel and deeply unpleasant creature,' the young man beside the fireplace spat forth his words.

'Ooh, what larks, the brawl continues!' The woman on the sofa curled her legs beneath her and clapped her hands. She had the air of one more accustomed to the finer things in life. Her hair was perfectly coiffed, and upon her forefinger glinted an imperious ring. Sapphire, by the looks of it. 'Mrs Thewley, I'm Winifred

Roberts – hotel correspondent for *Home and Country*. I came here to review dear old Charles's latest reckless venture, expecting it to be a damp squib full of floating Tarot cards and rattling tables. But I find myself rather enjoying the blood sport on offer. Namely: ruffling the Spiritualist feathers of Mr Hammond here and his awfully protective son.'

Winifred Roberts shook Mrs Thewley's hand and waved at Charles, signalling that her drink was in need of replenishment.

Kenneth Hammond by the fireplace snorted. 'If by "ruffling feathers", you mean deriving pleasure from mercilessly poking fun at a man still grieving the loss of his wife – *my mother* – then yes, you have been ruffling some bloody feathers.'

At this, the young man's father intervened in a bid to pour cold water on the sparring between his son and Winifred Roberts.

'Pleasure to meet you, Mrs Thewley,' he began warmly. 'Raymond Hammond. And this is Kenneth. He's feeling rather geed up at present, for which I apologise. Kenneth's back from university for the holidays, so we thought we'd take a trip – something a bit different, you know, something out of the ordinary.'

Winifred Roberts had turned her sneering gaze to Daphne now.

'Now *you* appear to be a rather . . . *cosmopolitan* creature. Do introduce us, Charles.'

Charles gestured towards Daphne with his cane. 'I forget myself, I do apologise! This', he said proudly, 'is Daphne King. My dear cousin's dearest friend, companion and confidante. Veronica, said cousin, is a playwright, a rather successful one of late, she's taking New York by storm as we speak.'

This impressed Winifred Roberts, who raised her eyebrows and nodded approvingly. 'New York bounding, you say? And what is it that you do, Miss King? Something . . . exciting and *modern*, judging by your apparel?'

Charles handed Daphne a gin and began to reply, 'Daphne here is *tremendously* successful, a *tremendous* success she really is. Ever heard of Sherlock Holmes? Well, he hasn't a leg to stand on next to our dear Daphne.'

Daphne sipped her drink and patted Charles on the shoulder. Not long ago, she would have blushed and modestly swatted away compliments about her investigative skills. Over the last few months, however, Daphne had started to embrace such praise. She was damned good at her job – why should she retreat from the objective truth of this? It was an ethos that Veronica had been cultivating in her since they had met last Christmas: no more shrinking violets, Daphne. She sipped and replied,

'To your question, Miss Roberts. I'm an investigative reporter for the *Chronicle*. Exciting, yes, but modern, no: people have been committing crimes since time immemorial – and getting caught because of their laziness or arrogance or incompetence.'

'Or because they're being investigated by a genius with a knack for unravelling mysteries, uncovering dark motives and unveiling the truth of human nature,' Charles added, tapping the top of his cane merrily.

'Well, well, well,' Mrs Thewley intoned, stroking Duke and smiling broadly. 'You and I might have rather a lot in common, Miss King.'

Daphne tilted her head quizzically. 'Oh?'

Mrs Thewley continued, her eyes twinkling. 'Yes, I too enjoy a spot of . . . fact-finding. Duke and I enjoy touring the country's . . . more supernatural establishments, prodding and prising things open. Generally causing trouble and opening all sorts of cans of worms. So what better way to usher in the festive season than a séance with the famed Madame Marla?'

Mrs Thewley chuckled to herself as Daphne glanced at Charles. He gave an exaggerated eye-roll.

'It's true: Mrs Amelia Thewley is, shall we say, quite a *name* amongst those of us in the paranormal business. There are those in the Spiritualist community who'd be spitting feathers if they knew I'd invited Mrs Thewley here; certain individuals who would call Mrs Thewley an interfering old so-and-so. I, on the other hand,' Charles now bowed flamboyantly, 'say that she is a practical-minded – if sometimes bloody-minded – pursuer of truth, and that is why she is welcome here at Maybridge Castle, where I suspect that our other-worldly friends might persuade her to see the world differently.'

Daphne looked around the room once more. At Eleanor Beaumont, who had seated herself in an armchair near the fireplace and whose smile remained undimmed, guilelessly happy with her lot. John Beaumont, meanwhile, rested his hand on his wife's shoulder, the sweat on his forehead visible once more. Neither of the Hammonds were making a particularly convincing show of appearing at ease in the room. Winifred Roberts, of course. Daphne had encountered her sort before: society types for whom gossip is like oxygen, and in whom very little trust can be placed. It was only then that Daphne realised that there was one further person in the room. So inconspicuous and unprepossessing that her presence had gone entirely undetected by Daphne until now. In the corner, intently scrubbing a spot on the velvet curtain, was the woman that Charles had introduced her to earlier: Mrs Moore.

'What a fascinating little hodgepodge you've assembled here, Charles,' Daphne commented amiably as her host delivered another gin to her and to Mrs Thewley.

'Well, only the crème de la crème for the grand open-ing of Maybridge Castle,' he chuckled, moving away to pour more sherry into Winifred Roberts's glass.

'I'll drink to that!' Winifred hooted.

The earlier episode of antagonism between Winifred and Kenneth seemed to have subsided after Daphne's arrival with Mrs Thewley and the Beaumonts – much to Charles's evident relief. He stood before the group in his rumpled corduroy suit, the elbows and knees worn to a shine. Clearing his throat, he began to outline the itiner-ary for the weekend: tomorrow, Saturday, would offer up the scintillatingly spine-chilling activities of Tarot card readings and a séance. These were courtesy of Mes-dames Marla and Thelma, the renowned clairvoyants of Asperdale. In addition, the guests would have the opportunity to roam the woodland in the grounds, the site said to be the burial grounds for women executed during the gruesome witch trials of some centuries ago. Their second day at Maybridge Castle would afford the guests the chance to explore the surrounding area, per-haps skipping through bogs to reach the local antique emporium, or indeed a bracing, frost-bitten walk to the beach.

'And fear not: in amongst all of the communing with spirits from the other side, there'll be lashings of the more traditional spirits to give us courage,' Charles raised his glass, 'And, naturally, banquets of all manner laid on by Mrs Moore, breakfast, noon and night.'

Murmurs of approval followed Charles's announcement. Winifred proclaimed, 'Well, the readers of *Town and Country* will be captivated by my report. Let's just hope you can keep the place afloat long enough for anyone else to visit, eh Charles.'

Their host smiled politely. 'No need for any concerns – or digs – Winifred. This isn't another of my ill-considered enterprises, I can promise you that. Maybridge Castle will be the making of me, you mark my words.' There was an unexpected sharpness to Charles's utterance, an air of irritability that Daphne hadn't noticed in him before now.

Burblings of chitchat and polite conversation simmered around the room, while Charles had set the gramophone to play some Christmas carols – rather prematurely, Daphne thought, seeing as it was still another ten days before Christmas itself. Eleanor Beaumont was providing Winifred with the details of her wedding day, ignorant of the expression of disdain that Winifred had plastered upon her face. The surly figure of Kenneth Hammond stood alone in his spot by the fireplace, brow furrowed, his face untroubled by a smile. Daphne and Mrs Thewley, meanwhile, were ensconced in conversation with the affable Raymond Hammond and the skittish John Beaumont.

'Now, forgive me, Mr Beaumont – ah, hang on, should I be addressing you as Mr or Dr?' Mrs Thewley said, removing her cardigan. 'I say, this gin does give one a rather pleasant warming sensation doesn't it?'

John Beaumont ran his hand through his thinning hair and replied, 'Oh, call me John, please. No need to stand on ceremony, Mrs Thewley.'

'If you insist,' she answered. 'Now, forgive me, John – but I have the most stubborn verruca at the moment. Suspect I picked it up at the Hampstead ponds. Possibly the Fulham baths. In any case, the bugger's been there about six weeks or so. Don't suppose you can offer any doctorly advice?'

For the first time in the hour or so that Daphne had been in John's presence, he smiled. Or, rather, half-smiled. 'I'm afraid I rather swerve away from doling out medical guidance when I'm off the clock – and especially when I'm on the sauce,' he explained, tipping his gin tumbler.

Raymond Hammond chuckled. 'Quite right too, John. And where is it that you're on the clock? Did Charles say it was Surbiton?'

John's half-smile disappeared. He answered tightly, throwing a glance at his wife, who was still engrossed in her own story. 'Thereabouts.'

Daphne observed as Mrs Thewley swooped in and rescued Raymond from the terseness that had descended.

'Well, my verruca will be delighted to be seeing in yuletide, possibly even the new year. Starting 1937 with a virally compromised foot; it's not the worst that's happened to me, I can tell you that.'

Mrs Thewley really did have a talent for setting others at ease, Daphne noted. A valuable asset in social situations, of course, but even more vital when it came to her own line of business. Daphne had been working hard on her ability to come off as charming and friendly, rather than forthright and tenacious. The results had been mixed, but generally speaking, she was making a rather good fist of it. As she rolled up the sleeves of her blouse (it was becoming rather warm in the room), she noticed that poor Mrs Moore was still scrubbing away at the curtain.

Daphne approached her, gin in hand. 'That's a stubborn one!'

Mrs Moore looked up with a start and her eyes darted quickly around the room. It was highly unusual, Daphne knew, for a guest to choose to interact so gaily and freely with domestic staff. But hooey to that – Charles had introduced them earlier. And besides, it had always left a bad taste in Daphne's mouth when, at the society parties she now frequented with Veronica, she saw the way others treated house staff as if they were entirely invisible. Veronica always laughed at this, saying that 'making small talk with the help does not a revolutionary make'.

Daphne continued, 'Have you tried lemon and baking powder? Works wonderfully on buggers like that.'

The woman shook her head. Her discomfort was evident, and her eyes remained fixed to a spot on the floor. Daphne cleared her throat. 'Well, it's a tried and tested favourite, daresay it'll save you all this elbow grease.'

Giving an awkward curtsy, Mrs Moore made her way to the door.

'Golly, Daphne,' Charles called over to her. 'Do stop pestering poor Mrs Moore – she's enough on her plate running this place without you grilling her!'

9

Against all odds, Daphne was enjoying herself tremendously. The sherry was flowing, the fire was blazing, and, despite her earlier misgivings about the Christmas carols, she found herself gently humming along to the tunes issuing forth from the gramophones. And there was something in the air. Something she couldn't quite put her finger on. She caught Mrs Thewley's eye. The white-haired lady was looking around the room silently, a tranquil smile upon her face. Daphne thought a private confabulation with Mrs Thewley might be in order at some point. She had the sense that the old lady might have some insightful observations about their fellow guests – observations which might shed light on those whispers in the corridor from earlier in the evening.

For now, however, Daphne was content to listen to Winifred Roberts's speechifying. 'Oh it's sublime, the hotel-reviewing game. Swoop in, lap up the champagne, make a couple of demands – a different pillow, if you please, this toast is woefully pale, don't you know – then off you pop back home. *Gloria in labore* – that was my school motto. *Glory through hard work*, my hat. Glory through having a bloody lovely time, that's my new motto. And I'll tell you what, this job's a damned sight more glamorous than my previous incarnation as Old Bailey correspondent at some old rag.'

'Old Bailey?' Daphne interjected. 'You must have seen your share of intriguing cases, no?'

'Pah! Chance would be a fine bloody thing,' Winifred replied. 'There for ten years, and did I cover any macabre murders or organised criminal activities of an elaborate and unprecedented nature? Did I heck. The closest I got was that chancer who was scurrying around town ingratiating himself with any rich old fool silly enough to take him in. You know the sort: sidles up to moneyed dodders, cons them then does a runner.'

Daphne's interest was piqued. She had a vague memory of that story. All very sad, she seemed to recall. A scam artist blazing a trail around the more privileged parts of London, the elderly rich being left nigh-on penniless and without an ounce of dignity.

'Oh yes,' she replied. 'Wasn't there that old chap who thought he was investing in a new shipping company, promised the next Titanic, only . . . less sinkable? And then it transpired that he'd funnelled his money directly into the pocket of the charlatan?'

At that, a cough beside the door announced the arrival of Charles's man, Mr Moore. Evidently a jack-of-all-trades, he served as chauffeur, odd-job man and butler.

'A ... Dr Rackham is here, Mr Howton,' Moore announced, before retreating.

Charles clapped his hands once more. 'Splendid! Our final guest!'

The woman Moore had introduced stepped into the drawing room. Rather short, an abundance of faded blonde hair pulled roughly into an unkempt bun, she smiled nervously, her hands fidgeting before her. Like Winifred Roberts, she appeared to be somewhere in her forties. The woman's heavy plaid skirt might, Daphne thought, have been emerald green at some point in its past, but now appeared the colour of stale pea soup. The woman's jittery demeanour and toothsome smile made Daphne think of a timid pet rabbit she had had as a girl. Poor Snowy, forever on edge. The woman said, 'Hello all, how lovely to be here. A merry Christmas – oh gosh, feels funny to be saying that, I've been so awfully busy that I've barely had time to even think about it all. And now here I am, all these carols, these wonderfully ... unique ... jellies.'

'And that's just the start of all the seasonal goodies, you

mark my words,' Charles assured her, sweeping a glass of sherry into her hand. 'Now, everyone, we have amongst us an esteemed academic, one of the brightest minds at work in the historical field.'

As he had when introducing Daphne to the group, Charles beamed with pride as he explained that Dr Helena Rackham was a highly respected scholar of the witch-hunts. 'Currently based at – Edinburgh University, if I recall correctly?'

'Yes, quite. Jolly excited to see the graves – absolutely chomping at the bit to get out there, have a poke around. Oh gosh, that's rather macabre of me, isn't it?' Dr Rackham flushed slightly.

'A wonderfully mousy and joyously grisly boffin to add to our motley crew,' Winifred declared, raising her gin. 'You'll fit in splendidly!'

Daphne watched as Dr Rackham smiled benevolently at Winifred. A second or two passed, however, before uncertainty seemed to creep into her smile. A flicker of distrust flashed across her face. Her ambivalent eyes darted towards the watchful eyes of Daphne, who stood to shake her hand.

Introductions made, glasses drained, the first activity of the stay was announced: a game of murder in the dark.

'Now, for the uninitiated,' Charles explained. 'The game works thusly. The lights will be extinguished throughout the castle. One of us will be named the murderer. When my man Moore rings the bell and makes the opening declaration – for yes, there is an opening declaration – everyone else will scatter themselves about the castle, to be hunted – in pitch dark – by the murderer. If found, you must scream so that we know that one amongst us has fallen. And so it continues until Moore rings the bell after precisely thirty minutes of hunting. And then to dinner!'

Charles's zeal was infectious, and Daphne found herself giggling as though she were Mrs Eleanor Beaumont. Mrs Thewley was also brimming with enthusiasm about the endeavour. Having assured all assembled that yes, she and Duke would be able to participate in the game ('I'm seventy-five, not dead!'), Mrs Thewley volunteered to be the murderer.

'Though I might appreciate a little in the way of assistance,' she explained. 'Miss King – I don't suppose you'd mind acting as . . . deputy murderer?'

Daphne replied that she'd be only too happy, just as long as Duke, who was eyeing her warily, didn't feel put out by the intrusion.

Charles suggested a mock round of the game to familiarise the attendees with the rules and ambience.

'It can get rather . . . hairy,' Charles explained. 'And Mrs Thewley, as much as I admire your game nature, I must admit to feeling slightly trepidatious about your groping your way around the entire house in the dark – even in the company of your very competent assistant.'

Mrs Thewley was about to protest but Charles would not countenance it. 'Let's begin by confining ourselves merely to this room.'

There was a collective groan.

'Come now, Charles,' came Raymond's gentle reprimand. 'We're all grown-ups, we can manage it!'

'Hear, hear,' drawled Winifred. 'If we must indulge you in this child's play, then at least let us do it properly.'

Charles, however, was adamant. He shook his head and, waggling one finger chastisingly, added, 'One mustn't run before one can walk. That way disaster lies.'

And so it was that the guests were instructed to remain where they were while Charles extinguished the lights in the room.

It was an oddly intimate experience. In such close confines, Daphne could hear the others breathing. A sniffle from someone – Raymond? A stifled hiccup – Eleanor Beaumont, she suspected. A rat-a-tat-tat sneeze. But was that from within the room, or outside it?

Daphne felt something warm and soft brush against her leg and, in a reflexive act that embarrassed her seconds later, she involuntarily let out a yelp and kicked at the presence.

A huge yowl was heard. Duke.

'Oh bloody hell!' Daphne said aloud. 'Duke, I'm very sorry! Mrs Thewley – do you think he's hurt?'

There was a shuffling in the room. Other than that, silence in the darkness.

'Mrs Thewley?' Daphne hissed.

The skin on the back of her neck prickled. Where was Mrs Thewley?

Daphne took one tentative step forward, her hands blindly feeling out ahead of her.

A cough. Followed by a splutter. Choking? Then a thud. A rattling breathing.

Panic flooded through Daphne. This was no game.

'Right, I'm turning on that light, nobody move!' With a speed and confidence that surprised even Daphne, she somehow crashed her way around any obstacles and slammed the light switch on.

Ready for whatever sight might be waiting for her, she peered at the room. And immediately regretted her actions.

'My dear,' Mrs Thewley said. 'You look like you've seen a ghost. Whatever is the matter?'

The other guests variously displayed expressions of bemusement and irritation.

'I say, Daphne,' came Charles's strained voice, as he heaved himself up from the floor, leaning heavily upon his cane. 'Veronica said you needed a holiday, but I'd no idea your nerves were, ahh, shall we say ... this cranked up.'

Daphne attempted to regain her composure. It was a game, you ninny, she thought. Mrs Thewley murdered Charles. Charles was pretending to be dead.

'I – I – it just sounded like ...' she stammered, smoothing down her blouse in feigned nonchalance.

A smirk danced upon Winifred Roberts's face.

'Oh dear me, Miss King, it seems as though the life of crime is taking its toll on your delicate disposition. Just a silly game, not a matter of life and death,' she said.

Charles hobbled to Daphne and put his arm around her. 'Well, I for one am glad to have dear Daphne on guard here. No crooks shall pass undetected with her on watch. Now. Shall we play properly? Venture out of this drawing room?'

The other guests limbered up while the lights were being put out. Even the surly Kenneth Hammond looked eager to play. Eleanor clasped her husband's hand and cackled giddily, while John himself was occupied by picking at an unsightly hangnail on his thumb. Winifred Roberts snuck to the drinks cabinet for one further sherry as Dr Helena Rackham gabbled cheerfully if inanely about Duke's docility.

Mr Moore opened the door and stepped in grandly. Wordlessly, he rang the bell and announced: 'There's been a murder.'

At that, the guests dispersed and Mrs Thewley, Daphne and Duke lay in wait.

10

At first, Daphne found herself most unsettled by the darkness. Dense and impenetrable, it seemed to create an invisible barrier between her and her surroundings. Duke instinctively took the lead, and she and Mrs Thewley followed. Duke let out a brief miaow, as if signalling that the path ahead was clear. Then, it was the silence that was unnerving. Not a sound anywhere. It was as if the castle had been submerged in a barrel of thick tar.

'Buck up, Amelia,' Daphne heard Mrs Thewley whispering to herself.

'Everything okay, Mrs Thewley?' she asked, waving her arms in front of her as they continued stepping forward.

A pause.

'Yes, quite fine, thank you, Miss King. Rather more silent and dark than I was anticipating, that's all!' came her companion's reply.

'The darkness is quite some—' Daphne began, but was interrupted.

By a scream.

'Who the devil was that?' hissed Mrs Thewley.

It was impossible to say.

The guests had all scattered so quickly, it could be coming from anywhere. One thing was for certain, though. It was a woman's voice.

Daphne called out, 'Hello? Is – is anyone hurt? Everyone okay?'

No reply. She staggered forward. Where the bloody hell was the light switch? She hadn't memorised their positions. Bloody idiot. If only she had taken up smoking, a lighter would be rather helpful at this point in time.

Her hearing felt sharpened. She could make out a wailing sound. Distress? Injury? Fear?

Daphne felt her way along the corridor and, judging from the aromas that were growing stronger, had made her way to the kitchen. She groped along the wall and there it was: the light switch. Flicking it on, she cast her eyes about the room. It wasn't the kitchen after all. Daphne's senses had been entirely discombobulated by the darkness. Disoriented, she and Mrs Thewley had become turned around in the dark, and were back in the drawing room, next to the table filled with jellies.

Eleanor Beaumont was standing there, a look of disgust upon her face.

'What is it, Eleanor?' Daphne demanded. 'What's happened?'

Eleanor held up her hands. They were covered in a red substance.

'It's all over the back of my skirt,' she wailed. 'How am I going to get this out?'

Daphne came closer.

A plate lay on the floor, its contents destroyed and crushed. It was the jelly. Eleanor Beaumont had somehow sat in the jelly.

Daphne rolled her eyes. 'Baking soda, warmish water. Out in a jiffy.'

Mrs Thewley had entered the room. 'Oh dear, oh dear. Jelly on a wool skirt, now that is something to scream about, duckie. But what say we get on with this game, eh?'

And so the game continued. But it was only a few minutes, however, before another scream came. This time, it was a scream that ripped through the castle.

It was not the scream of a tipsy guest who had misunderstood the silly rules of this silly game.

Or the scream of a clumsy guest who had fallen into a plate of jelly.

Blood-curdling and terrifying, it was like a shard of ice hurled into the heart of the castle.

Daphne stood stock still. Panicking would solve nothing.

'Stay here, Mrs Thewley,' she said, no longer whispering. 'I'll be back.'

Where had the scream come from? Breathing steadily, one hand against the wall, the other before her, Daphne shuffled towards the centre of the castle.

She could make out a light before her, at the end of a corridor. A light that hadn't been extinguished.

She made her way to the light. It was coming from the cellar door.

She stood at the top of the stairs to the cellar and saw it.

A body. Limbs twisted, blood pooling about it.

The body of Winifred Roberts.

11

It was not the first time that Daphne had happened upon a gruesome scene. Nor would it be the last. Nonetheless, exposure to crime and violence and death did nothing to diminish the shock she experienced when such an episode arose.

First things first. She needed to act quickly, and she needed to act decisively. Daphne descended into the cellar and approached Winifred Roberts, who was, she ascertained, most decidedly dead. Daphne looked back up the stairs. There were only ten or so, not an extensive flight. Winifred Roberts must have fallen with quite some propulsion to have landed so forcefully. Daphne frowned. Then there was the matter of the blood; there was an awful lot of it. An *awful* lot of it, Daphne reflected. But where was it coming from? Daphne knew that she mustn't move Winifred's body; she must leave the scene intact for the arrival of the police. Which would happen in due course – once Daphne had had time to conduct her own initial observations of the blood-soaked area of the cellar floor.

Carefully, Daphne tiptoed her way around Winifred's body, peering closely to determine the source of the blood.

Aha.

There it was.

Head wound.

A very deep head wound on the left side of her skull.

The frown on Daphne's face intensified. She was no doctor, no police detective (a fact that innumerable doctors and police detectives had reminded her of in exasperation over the last year), but her instincts were muttering that there was something amiss with this injury. She cast about in her mind, fumbling for the connection she was trying to make. The wound to Winifred's head was deep, a gash that reminded her of ... where was it? What was it? Come on, Daphne, she thought. Then it came to her: in June, she had written about the Seymour murder. Jimmy Seymour, a publican in west London, had been hit over the head with a golf club. Daphne had seen the photographs taken at the time – she wheeled them out of her long-time friend, Inspector Marklow – and the gash created by the golf club was alarmingly similar to the wound she could see on Winifred Roberts's head.

It was a wound produced not by a skull slamming on

to a cellar floor, but rather by the strike of an implement. The violent strike of an implement.

Daphne knew that she had only minutes before one of the other guests would find the light emitted by the open cellar door. She looked around her. Was there anything else she needed to notice, any other details that, nondescript now, would crystallise into something revealing, something important, later?

She made herself look again at Winifred Roberts, the unnatural splaying of her limbs and the look of terror upon her lifeless face. Daphne had resolved that she must never harden herself against the realities of death. The realities of . . . murder.

Winifred's blouse was stained crimson, a red sliver of blood emerging also from her lips. Daphne hovered hesitantly. What else, she thought. She frowned, imploring herself to apply those observational skills that Veronica mocked – but admired.

Aha. There it was. Winifred's forefinger. It was bare. The sapphire ring was gone.

Daphne's eyes darted about the cellar floor. Could it have been dislodged in her fall? Skittered into a nook somewhere? Might she have taken it off before playing the game? Both unlikely explanations.

No, Daphne thought. The ring was missing because it had been removed. Not by Winifred Roberts.

Taking a deep breath, she stepped over the dead body and made her way back up the stairs just in time to be met by Kenneth Hammond, the young man so protective of his father earlier – the man who had spoken to Winifred Roberts with such anger.

'What the bloody hell's going on?' he asked, panting slightly. 'Where – who screamed?'

Daphne stepped aside and gestured to the cellar.

'Winifred Roberts screamed. She's dead.'

Kenneth Hammond's eyes widened and he brought his hand to his mouth.

Daphne groped on the wall, searching for a light switch. When she found it, the room was flooded with light. To her surprise, it was the kitchen. That game had entirely disoriented her – she had had no idea where in the castle she was stumbling into.

Daphne knew the steps that now needed to be taken. As loudly as she could, she shouted, 'The game is over! The game is over! Winifred is dead!'

She found herself almost tempted to repeat the opening declaration of the game – but to proclaim that there'd been a murder might be to set the cat amongst the pigeons, as it were. No, for now, she needed the other guests to emerge and she needed them to do so with as little information as possible.

Daphne glanced about the kitchen. Was there anything

out of place, anything peculiar? She scratched her head and realised the attempt to scrutinise the kitchen would be nigh-on futile. No, more useful would be to ensure that she could instead turn her scrutiny to the other guests. Kenneth Hammond had backed away from the cellar door and was propping himself against the large table in the middle of the kitchen.

'She – she fell down the stairs? What a bloody clumsy way to go,' he was muttering. 'I thought she was lady of the manor.'

'Mr Hammond – Kenneth. I'm not interested in your opinions about Winifred Roberts and the manner of her untimely end,' Daphne said coolly. She was, of course, most terribly interested in his opinions on Winifred Roberts and the manner of her untimely end, but now was not the moment. 'What I am interested in, however, is you making yourself useful. Go and call the police. The telephone is in the hallway, the main hallway. I'll rally the others.'

The gangly young man looked chastened and nodded weakly. Daphne took one final glance at the body in the cellar, then set about gathering her fellow guests.

12

No gramophone blared in the drawing room now, as it had done just hours earlier. No conversational to-ing and fro-ing, no smiles and small talk.

Daphne looked at the assembled guests, taking the measure of them all. She had gone to find Mrs Thewley first, of course. The woman had, as Daphne suspected she might, not heeded Daphne's words in the slightest. Contrary to Daphne's instructions, she had not remained stock still but instead had attempted to make her way to the source of the scream as well. Duly reprimanded by Daphne, Mrs Thewley had told her in no uncertain terms that she was a woman of action, not a woman to keep still and hide. Now, she was on the sofa, Duke curled up next to her – both of them looking inscrutable and forbidding. Daphne liked Mrs Thewley more and more with every passing moment. She was quite the best feature of Maybridge Castle so far, alongside the woollen Christmas tree bats and the array of objets.

The Beaumonts were in two chairs beside the fire. Eleanor Beaumont was sniffling uncontrollably, while her husband sat motionless beside her. Helena Rackham had spluttered manifold 'goshes' of varying pitches and intonations when Daphne had found her, and was now pacing beside the window. Daphne watched in fascination as Helena repeatedly tapped her teeth with her forefinger, a syncopated tic that never faltered.

Raymond Hammond stood by the mantelpiece, pipe in one hand. The stockings hanging there looked incongruous now, an emblem of jollity that had no place here any more. He was gazing into the fire, as if oblivious to the figures around him. His son Kenneth, meanwhile, was picking at a thread where he was sitting on the arm of the sofa.

Crikey, Daphne thought. This lot are going to keep me busy.

Charles flung open the door to the drawing room, Mr Moore following just behind him. He limped to the hearth, and cleared his throat. An alarming pallor had settled upon his face. Daphne stood.

'My – my sincerest apologies,' he began. Everyone looked up. 'What a . . . tragic, dismal way for the evening to unfold. Thank you all for your patience while we await the local police. They should be here imminently, I'm sure.'

He cast his eyes around the room. Nobody appeared certain about what to say – or whether to say anything.

Charles took a deep breath. 'I – this – this really isn't . . . perhaps we can—'

This was a worrying sight. Although Daphne had only known Charles for a year, and only then met him at various functions of Veronica's family, she had never seen him like this. Cousin Charles the loquacious and charismatic maverick of the family, Cousin Charles, who only had to tip his cane at a barman in his favourite pub to be served his favourite tipple, Cousin Charles who—

Charles's cane. Daphne thought. Where was Charles's cane?

'I – I must – I really must – apologise again – poor, poor Winifred . . .' Charles was continuing to gabble. 'This wasn't what . . .'

Charles didn't finish his sentence, however, for with that, he stumbled sideways unsteadily. Raymond Hammond dropped his pipe and, with both hands, gripped Charles under his arms.

Daphne rushed forwards. 'Charles! Charles, let's sit you down.'

John Beaumont sprang from the chair next to his wife and helped Daphne and Raymond manoeuvre Charles on to the sofa.

He was breathing quickly, blinking rapidly. 'My pills – get my pills, Moore – get my pills.'

Moore nodded, but just as he turned to leave the room, the doorbell clanged loudly.

'The police,' Moore stated. 'I ought to tell them what's what. Regarding the incident.'

Daphne, crouched now by Charles's side, glanced up at Moore. 'And the pills? I rather think Charles ought to have them pronto, don't you? Perhaps if I go—'

Dr Beaumont interjected, 'Please – Miss King – I feel . . . like something of a spare part here. Let me fetch the pills. Mr Moore – their whereabouts?'

Mr Moore's eyes narrowed, as if assessing whether Dr Beaumont could be trusted with this role. 'Cabinet in the bathroom adjoining Mr Howton's chambers. Third floor. I forget their name, at present, but they're for his ticker – I assume you'll know them when you see them, being a medical man?'

Daphne was startled. Moore's verbosity was highly unexpected. At this, Dr Beaumont and Mr Moore both left the drawing room.

She knelt by Charles's side, clutching his hand.

'You're all right, Charles, you're all right,' she said. 'The pills are on their way, you've had a shock, a very nasty shock.'

'I'll say!' came a wail from Eleanor Beaumont. 'That poor woman, dead at the bottom of some horrible old stairs. That poor, poor woman!'

Eleanor burst into sobbing once more, tears streaming down her already sodden face. Daphne frowned in exasperation. Had Eleanor Beaumont quite lost her head? She would have to say something to this woman; wailing and gnashing her teeth would do good to neither man nor beast.

'Now, now, Mrs Beaumont,' Mrs Thewley said. 'It's an unpleasant business, I'll grant you, but we must pull ourselves together in circumstances such as these. Best foot forward. I know your husband's a doctor, but I have a remedy that Dr Beaumont wouldn't be able to prescribe: a little practical potion I like to call strokies with Duke.'

At that, the tabby cat leapt from Mrs Thewley's lap on to Eleanor Beaumont's. She let out a little gasp of amusement, and began to stroke the purring cat, who was circling on her knees.

Daphne smiled. Mrs Thewley once again proving herself to have a far greater talent for diplomacy than her when confronted with tears.

'Yes, and what say we get you a hankie for ... that wet face of yours,' Daphne said, patting her trouser pockets in a search for her handkerchief.

Before she could find it, the housekeeper, Mrs Moore, stepped forward from the corner of the room. Had she been there the entire time? How the blazes did she do that? Daphne was speechless once more.

Mrs Moore handed Eleanor a handkerchief, giving a brief and awkward curtsey as she did. She then turned to the room and suggested that she fix a pot of tea – and would bring in a bottle of brandy for anyone whose nerves were so inclined.

Daphne had to give credit where credit was due: the Moores were certainly a helpful duo to have around in a crisis. Less, however, could be said of the other figures assembled in the drawing room. Eleanor Beaumont's seemingly uncontrollable sobs had given way to quiet squeals of delight as she stroked Duke and dangled her sodden handkerchief before him. Helena Rackham, hands visibly shaking, was repeatedly smoothing her plaid skirt. The Hammond men were engaged in a murmured conversation, inaudible to Daphne despite straining her ears in an attempt to snatch the gist of their discussion.

The door creaked open. Dr Beaumont walked in, an agitated look upon his face.

'Can't find the bloody pills – they're not there,' he spluttered in exasperation.

'Perhaps I should go and retrieve them myself,' Mr Moore appeared in the open doorway behind Dr Beaumont. 'The police have everything in hand.'

Charles let out a whimper. Daphne squeezed his hand and told Moore to be quick-sharp about getting those blasted pills. Dr Beaumont went and joined his wife, frowning slightly as Duke took a swipe at him. He hovered beside his wife, before clearing his throat.

'Charles, Miss King,' Dr Beaumont began, 'Although I failed to fetch the pills, please let me at least do something to help. I'd like to put myself to good use, speak to the police – shed what light I can on the events. If you're in agreement?'

He looked searchingly at the pair. Daphne hesitated. If anyone should go, it should of course be her. But she couldn't leave Charles while he was in this condition. She could imagine the conversation with Veronica: *Oh yes, I did leave Cousin Charles breathing heavily and looking as pale as a sheet, yes I thought he'd be fine with a room full of strangers, it was jolly sad he popped his clogs while I was snooping around with the local police.* Better not risk it, Daphne decided.

She glanced at Charles. The pallor of his face had

taken on an even more disconcerting green hue. Beads of sweat slid down his brow.

'Yes, very well, Dr Beaumont. Be as thorough as you can, and be as efficient as you can. As soon as Charles here is looking less . . . as soon as I can, I'll join you. I want to hear precisely what it is the police are thinking and doing.'

When Mrs Moore returned with the tea and the brandy, Daphne poured herself a large tumbler of the latter. She found it sharpened her senses, granted her a clarity of vision and purpose under circumstances of duress. To her pleasant surprise, Mrs Thewley joined her in the brandy – winking somewhat incongruously as she did so.

After a few moments, Charles began breathing more evenly, and Daphne squeezed his hand reassuringly.

Taking the final gulp of the tumbler, Daphne turned to Charles.

'Now you're feeling less . . . unsteady, Charles, I think I might go and see how the police are getting on with Dr Beaumont.' Daphne rose from her position on the floor beside him. 'See if there's anything I can – ah – assist them with.'

It was as she turned to the door that she heard Dr Beaumont's voice in the corridor outside. A reply came, followed by a sneeze. The door to the drawing room opened, and Dr Beaumont shuffled in, closing it behind him. His head was bowed slightly.

'Everything all right, Dr Beaumont?' she asked, her hands in her pockets as she approached him.

He turned around slowly, his face unreadable.

'The, uh, constabulary are on their way out, I believe.'

She glanced at her wristwatch. Twenty minutes or so had passed since their arrival.

'Already?' she asked incredulously. 'What did they say? What did they do? When are they coming back to collect the body?'

There was a pause before the doctor replied.

'He said she must have fallen down the stairs – no question of it, all said and done,' Dr Beaumont explained. 'He said . . . he said . . . he was going to take her away, said no need to come back.'

'Well, I'll see about that,' she muttered, rolling up her sleeves in anticipation of confronting this countryside constabulary and giving them a what for.

Daphne couldn't quite believe her ears. Naturally, she was accustomed to the ways of the London police. Perhaps here they conducted things differently. Didn't ask questions, didn't look for witnesses. Assumed a death to be an accidental tumble down some stairs when a chasm in the left side of the victim's skull suggested a very different story.

Just as she was about to leave the room, Charles moaned in pain. She hesitated. Veronica. She couldn't leave him there.

'Ohhh, fiddlesticks,' she uttered, surprising herself with such a quaint turn of phrase under such dire circumstances. She crouched by Charles's side once again for what seemed an eternity, soothing him while she herself grew more frustrated by the second.

She heard various bumps and crashes in the corridor. Another sneeze. Then the slamming of the heavy front door.

The door to the drawing room opened and Mr Moore appeared, a bottle of pills in his hand. Approaching Charles, he straightened his tie, and Daphne noticed a scuff on his white shirt. The pills must have been very hard to reach indeed.

Charles gratefully swallowed his pill, and with a 'there, there,' Daphne leapt to the doorway. Empty. Truly a haphazard way of policing.

Not only had the constabulary conducted a rather shambolic operation here, but Daphne also inwardly berated herself. Laughable work. To stay cocooned in the drawing room while Moore, unreadable yet efficient, Dr Beaumont, agitated and useless, were left to roam the castle and interact with the police? She could have kicked herself. A glance back at Charles, however, reminded Daphne that there were, lamentably, instances in which her professional responsibilities and instincts had to play second fiddle to other duties.

'Perhaps we ought to ask Mrs Moore to . . . clean the cellar,' Dr Beaumont said before walking past Daphne slowly, as if measuring out each step.

13

Daphne's first night at Maybridge Castle had been far more dramatic than she had bargained for. A few days in the countryside, a break from the tumult and the grime of London. Restorative and refreshing. Or so Veronica had promised so persuasively when cajoling Daphne into going.

She sat now at the small desk in her bedroom. She had cleared it of its Spiritualist guides, the anthology of ghost stories and the small glass jar containing one solitary dried thistle. She tapped her pen against her notebook, a habit that never failed to prompt sighs of exasperation from Veronica.

After the incident, a collective realisation of hunger had taken hold of the guests. Mrs Moore had obligingly presented various platters that she had prepared – some roast lamb, salmon en croute, veal loaf, trifle pudding – and they had joylessly shovelled down the food. All, of course, liberally washed down with some claret that

Charles opened. Daphne had then escorted Charles to his room, playing the role of caring cousin by proxy. He looked frailer than she'd ever seen him before. She had never been certain of his age, but he couldn't have been more than sixty. Yet, saying good night to him and watching him limp into his bedroom, Daphne saw Cousin Charles for the first time as an old man. Winifred's death had taken its toll. No wonder, she thought. Charles's ineptitude with money was a longstanding joke in his family. A joke that everyone laughed at outwardly, but she suspected that the merriment masked an embarrassment, a sense of shame at his reckless nature. Maybridge Castle was to be his redemption, proof that he did possess acumen – that he had harnessed an idea and was able to see it to successful fruition.

And now this. The first journalist here to review his venture had died. Fallen to her death in Maybridge Castle during a fatal game of murder in the dark. It was quite the story.

Daphne paused and replayed her thoughts: hotel reviewer plunges to her death while staying at England's first haunted hotel.

Minimal effort would be required to turn that into a headline. A very appealing headline at that. A headline which, she knew, would be splashed all over countless newspapers up and down the country. Then other journalists would come to Maybridge Castle, writing stories of their stays with the poltergeists and the spirits. Then the guests would come, wanting to tell their friends and family about how they stayed in the haunted death-drop hotel and survived it.

Could it be . . . ?

No. Daphne shook her head forcefully, wanting to banish the thought. No, that was quite enough of that malarkey.

There was that other question, however. The question of why Cousin Charles wasn't using his cane when he appeared after the game.

No, stop it, she urged herself. Stop playing silly buggers, Daphne.

Before she could grapple with her thoughts any longer, there was a light tapping at the door and an odd brushing sound. She glanced at her watch. It was eleven forty-five. Who could be knocking at this hour? She tightened her dressing gown and padded to the door, opening it a crack.

'Miss King,' came a whisper. 'It's me, Mrs Thewley.'

There was a small meow.

'And Duke.'

Relieved, Daphne opened the door and gestured for Mrs Thewley to enter. Duke looped himself around Daphne's legs as she walked, nearly tripping her up.

'That's a good sign: he only does that when he likes someone,' Mrs Thewley explained as she approached the chair beside the desk.

There being no other chairs in the room, Daphne perched on the edge of the bed. 'Mrs Thewley, I'm ashamed to admit that I'm unaccustomed to such late-night visitors.'

'Oh, I find that difficult to believe, duckie,' chuckled Mrs Thewley. 'What with this Veronica being a bohemian type, the mind boggles at all the high-jinks you must get up to in London.'

Against her will, Daphne blushed slightly. Mrs Thewley was quite the force to be reckoned with.

'Now, I've come to talk about this evening, dear,' Mrs Thewley continued, folding her hands on her lap. 'Usually, I confine my speculations to a chat with Duke – he has the most splendid judgement when it comes to these things.'

Daphne watched as Duke sat on the threadbare carpet and, leg hoisted, began to attend to his hygiene routine.

'I see,' she replied to Mrs Thewley, trying to suppress the note of excitement that was creeping into her voice. 'And what is it you'd like to discuss, Mrs Thewley?'

'Well, in the first instance, I'd rather like to hear your suspicions about what really happened,' Mrs Thewley said bluntly. 'I should find that very, very thrilling indeed.'

Daphne was taken aback. She began stuttering a demurral.

'Oh come, come, dear,' Mrs Thewley said. 'I know a canny operator when I see one, and you, Miss King, are one of the canniest I've encountered. You don't suffer fools, and neither do I. So.'

A grin of bemusement swept over Daphne's face. Here she was at a quarter to midnight, in the middle of the Cumbrian countryside, one woman dead, and an elderly Spiritualist-hunter sitting in her bedroom wanting her to spill the beans about her as-yet entirely nebulous hunches. Rarely did she divulge her early-stage speculations even to Veronica, much to her chagrin. She liked Mrs Thewley, truly she did, but to reveal anything now could lead to catastrophe.

'Mrs Thewley, I must say that I'm rather . . . flattered by your assessment of me,' she began. 'But I fear you may have me mistaken for someone of a far more . . . cynical outlook.'

'Oh poppycock. Miss King, I don't mince my words, and I sincerely believe that you don't either,' Mrs Thewley said lightly. 'There's something queer going on here, and I know that you think so too. I've seen the way you look at the others, you know what's what. And what's what is . . . that horrid woman didn't just fall down those stairs.'

Daphne bit her lip and stood up from the edge of the bed. An ally, a confidante could be helpful. Mrs Thewley was undoubtedly an intelligent woman; she could be an asset. Daphne had none of her usual associates about her – Veronica, Inspector Marklow, her contacts in the pubs, factories, streets of London – and she was on unfamiliar ground.

She sighed.

'No, I don't think that horrid woman did just fall down the stairs.'

And with that, Daphne explained to Mrs Thewley the head wound, the similarity to the Seymour golf-club murder. Mrs Thewley nodded along, while Duke continued his strict adherence to cleanliness standards.

'Now, loathe as I am to cry murder, I rather think that Winifred Roberts *was* murdered,' Daphne concluded. 'Why the police didn't hang about to ask anyone anything – well, that escapes me.'

'One rather supposes that the village constabulary might not be in the practice of exercising the sharpest sleuthing skills known to man,' Mrs Thewley agreed. 'Now, the question is, duckie, how are we going to get to the bottom of things?'

Daphne couldn't help but smile at the 'we.'

'I propose, Mrs Thewley,' she said, scooping Duke into her arms as she did, 'that we both get ourselves a good night's sleep. And that tomorrow, we go about our days with an unparalleled level of vigilance and insight.'

'Wonderful, dear,' Mrs Thewley replied. 'Vigilance and insight it is.'

14

The next morning, breakfast was a peculiar affair. Delicious, thanks to Mrs Moore's unwavering efforts. Fragrant kedgeree in a tureen in one corner (a Saturday morning tradition at Maybridge Castle, Charles explained), freshly baked soda bread and homemade butter in another. Charles had regained his strength and his composure, and was doing his utmost to distract his guests from the sense of shock and discomfort that had descended upon Maybridge Castle since Winifred Roberts's death.

Daphne entered the dining room to find him holding court among the rather despondent-looking guests.

'So it transpired that it was a badger all along! A *badger*, if you can believe it!' Charles gave a hearty laugh, while polite titters rippled around the table. Only Eleanor Beaumont seemed to have enjoyed the anecdote with any sincerity, and she wiped a tear from her eye with the handkerchief that Mrs Moore had lent her yesterday. It was heartening, Daphne supposed, to see it being put to a use that didn't involve excessive and, she felt, disingenuous, lachrymosity.

Daphne found a seat at the end of the table, and before she had even sat down, Mrs Moore had glided towards her, teapot in hand.

'Why thank you, Mrs Moore, how kind,' Daphne said. Mrs Moore's unwieldy curtsy made a reappearance before she glided out of the room.

Mrs Thewley was already seated next to Raymond Hammond, and both were spreading marmalade on to their toast. After greeting them, Daphne added a splash of milk to her tea and surveyed the room. One would be hard pressed to detect that one of their number had died just last night. The festive paper-chains still hung from the ceiling, the oranges studded with cloves were even more aromatic than the day before. Mrs Thewley quickly became engrossed in chitchat with Raymond Hammond; Daphne knew that she would be told anything of import from this conversation later.

Kenneth Hammond had not appeared for breakfast, Eleanor Beaumont was chatting animatedly with Charles while her husband listlessly moved scrambled eggs around on his plate with his fork.

That left . . .

'Oh gosh, good morning everyone, goodness me, hello!' Helena Rackham scurried into the dining room, greeting everyone in a timorous and apologetic tone. Her cardigan was fastened unevenly, buttons missed out here and there, while the hem of her woollen skirt appeared in need of stitching. Daphne never took appearances as weighty evidence of a person's character, but she had to admit that oftentimes it was useful to take such things into account.

Now that she had successfully entered the dining room and said her hellos, Helena appeared hesitant about how to proceed. Daphne saw her opportunity and waved for Helena to sit beside her. The woman's face registered a series of emotions – nervousness, apprehension, vague surprise – before she trotted round to the proffered seat.

At once, Mrs Moore appeared at her side, pouring the now rather lukewarm tea into her cup.

'Miss Rackham! What a delight,' Daphne said warmly. 'Charles has told me so much about you and your academic pursuits – how utterly *bewitching*!'

Though it wasn't wordplay that Daphne was terribly proud of, Helena giggled at the pun.

'Yes, I can't deny being completely *under the spell* of my studies,' Helena replied, clearly pleased as punch with having engaged in some badinage with Daphne. 'We're really only just scratching the surface of the witch-hunts – the brutality, the hysteria, the utter horrors of it all.'

Helena's gleeful smile was in comical discord with the sentiments she was alluding to.

'And now we think that the woodland here at May-bridge Castle is the burial site of a group of women found guilty of witchcraft in, we think, 1618,' Helena continued, taking a small sip of her tea. Daphne listened on, oddly enraptured by the passion with which this heretofore timid woman was holding forth. 'Imagine, the woodland at the very castle my dear old friend Charles buys! I was cock-a-hoop when I heard it, of course, absolutely over the moon. Charles is ever so generous, as I'm sure you already know, absolutely one in a million. Told me that I can come and stay whenever I need to, for my research.'

Daphne nodded, a wave of melancholy washing over her. Charles was indeed generous; generous to a fault, in fact. It was his naivety and good nature that had contrib-uted to his financial straits, 'lending' money here and there to help out a friend or two. Loans that, of course, he never saw returns on.

'And tell me, Miss Rackham—'

'Oh please, call me Helena – Miss Rackham is what my students in Edinburgh call me,' she demurred.

Daphne continued, 'Tell me, Helena, where might I be able to read some of your research? I find myself rather fascinated by the subject; it's not one I've a terrible amount of knowledge about, and to have it from the expert horse's mouth would be rather thrilling.'

In her year of investigating crime and rubbing shoulders with racketeers, thieves and murderers, Daphne had learnt many things. She had learnt that buying a steak and kidney pie for a small-time crook would do wonders for their volubility. She had learnt how to wade through the Scotch mist of a Soho drinking den and wade back out again unscathed. She had learnt how to eat scallops at Billingsgate Market at five o'clock in the morning without feeling queasy. But it was Mrs Thewley who had given her the proof of something that she'd long suspected: buttering people up made life a heck of a lot easier.

Helena nearly spat out her tea at Daphne's question. 'You'd – you'd like to *read* my work? You, Miss Daphne King, illustrious and intrepid crime reporter, would like to read my . . . research papers?'

Bingo, thought Daphne. If Helena Rackham had anything of interest to share about last night, Daphne would be able to winkle it out of her. After all, Daphne was now her self-professed acolyte and admirer.

Helena explained that, yes, as a matter of fact, she had one of her research papers with her – she wasn't, of course, in the habit of carting her work around with her on the off-chance that someone would ask to read it (a giggle as she said this), but as she was here on research business, it was only natural to bring her most recent work with her. In case the findings in the woodland called for any amendments or additions.

'Splendid,' Daphne replied. 'I shall snuggle up with it tonight for my bedtime reading.'

There came a clinking. Daphne looked up to see Charles standing, tapping a teaspoon against the side of his cup.

'Morning all, morning all,' he said, the frail and shaken man of last night seeming but an imagined phantom. 'What a joy it is to see you all here, all enjoying the delicious breakfast laid on by the wonderful Mrs Moore.'

Daphne scanned the room and noted that not *all* were there: young Kenneth Hammond was still nowhere to be seen.

'We do, as you'll remember, have a very busy day ahead of us. But before that, as your gracious host, I feel it behoves me to address something of an elephant in the room.'

Any jollity that a table festooned with marmalades, jams and scrambled eggs might have invoked now disappeared. All stared intently at Charles.

'I think it only fitting that we speak of the terrible tragedy that befell Miss Winifred Roberts last night. A terrible, terrible thing to happen.' As Charles continued, a faraway look descended upon him. His eyes were glassy, fixed on an indistinct point in the distance. 'It was an awful accident, truly, truly awful. But, as they say, the show must go on. Maybridge Castle has weathered many an unfortunate incident in its long and colourful past: and still it stands, still it survives. Let us raise a cup of tea – if that doesn't seem ridiculous – to Winifred Roberts.'

A chorus of her name echoed back at Charles.

Daphne could see, however, out of the corner of her eye that Helena Rackham had not raised her tea cup. Instead, she had started to tap her front teeth with her forefinger, as she had done last night. Hallo, thought Daphne. What have we here?

'Can I pass you any jams or marmalade, Helena?' she asked, apparently startling the woman.

'Oh! Oh, ah, no – no thank you,' Helena replied.

'Jolly sad thing to happen, can't quite believe it,' Daphne said casually, forcing a nonchalance into her voice as though she were merely commenting on the weather.

Helena made a vague murmur of agreement in return.

'She seemed like such a ... vibrant woman, by all accounts a formidable person,' Daphne continued tentatively. She mustn't push too hard, easy does it.

Was that a snort she heard? She looked at Helena's face. Her expression had darkened. Derision? Disdain?

'Vibrant.' Helena muttered, shaking her head.

'Sorry? I don't follow . . . ?' Daphne replied, smearing a dollop of marmalade on to her third slice of toast. All this subtle probing and prodding always made her hungry.

Helena Rackham placed her hands carefully on the tablecloth, one on either side of her plate. 'All I mean to say is . . . just because the woman is dead, it doesn't necessarily follow that we ought to . . . feel sad.'

Well, well. Daphne thought. What have we here? She often found that allowing people the time and space to fill silences yielded extraordinary results. There was a time for poking, for following a comment with a seemingly guileless question – but there was also a time for sitting back, taking a bite of toast and waiting. Simply waiting.

'What I mean is,' Helena continued, 'why mourn someone who wasn't a terribly nice person? Who was, on the contrary, a rather cruel person. Someone who didn't give two hoots for other people's feelings. It feels rather . . . deceitful to mourn a person like that. Rather . . . vexatious, to indulge in cheap sentiment. In my opinion.' Helena's hands had remained fixed in place as she said this. Her voice had risen to such a level that the other guests had stopped their various conversations and had heard every word she had uttered.

'Was she – a rather cruel person?' Daphne asked calmly, still imbuing her voice with the insouciance of one possessed by friendly curiosity, rather than one engaged in professional enquiries.

A pause. Daphne watched Helena narrowly, but, surprisingly, she betrayed no sign of discomposure.

'So I understand. From ... from the way I've been told that she spoke to Mr Hammond here and his son,' Helena replied. 'And yes, yes I think I will have some of that marmalade, thank you, Miss Ki—Daphne.'

Passing the jar, Daphne glanced at Mrs Thewley. She was wearing an expression of wry bemusement and winked surreptitiously at Daphne.

The game truly was afoot.

'Now, is anyone going to finish these scrambled eggs, or do I have collective permission to donate them to Duke? He is on his holidays, after all.' Mrs Thewley glanced around the room before scraping the eggs on to a side plate ready for conveyance up to her bedroom.

15

As instructed by their host, after breakfast the guests prepared themselves for an expedition into the outside: namely, a short ramble through the woodland in the castle's grounds.

Daphne had retrieved her coat, a heavy, dark-brown trench coat that Veronica had bought her in January. Daphne had deemed her old coat perfectly wearable, but, according to Veronica, perfectly wearable was not going to cut the mustard for Daphne King, investigative reporter at large.

She came back downstairs to find the hallway empty. Everyone must be taking a rather longer time getting themselves ready for the ramble. A wooden sideboard stood on one side of the hallway. It was dotted with various trinkets and curios: a bundle of crisp sage, the ends slightly singed (Charles had told her about the cleansing ceremonies he held every week); a few seashells, presumably foraged from the beach that lay a mile or so away; and a crystal ball, which Daphne judged was taking things a little too far.

Upon a small table nearby sat the telephone and a vase containing dried thistles like those in her bedroom. The drawing room was the first room along the hallway, followed by the dining room. A parlour lay beyond that, though Daphne had yet to spend any time in this room. And at the end of the hallway, at the back of the house, was the kitchen. Daphne could hear the rattling and clanging of pots and pans. Mrs Moore must be preparing their lunch already.

As Daphne was sniffing the bundle of sage on the dresser (a rather acrid and noxious scent; no wonder the evil spirits fled from it, she thought), there came a scratching sound. Tentative at first, it grew louder and more rhythmic. She placed the sage back on its shelf and listened. It was coming from the front door. The large brass key to the door sat in a pot on the dresser, so Daphne lifted it and opened the door with some effort – to be met with an eager Duke, who galloped past her and straight up the stairs.

'How did you get out there, you little rascal?' she found herself asking the rapidly retreating cat.

Now that the door was open, Daphne decided to step outside and survey the grounds properly in daylight. The day was a sharp and bright one, gone the gloomy clouds and the indecisive drizzle of yesterday. She pulled her coat tight about her against the shards of cold air. Directly ahead of the castle door were the stables, which were in a sorry state of disrepair. Daphne peeked in and saw rotting crates, a pile of crumbling bricks, along with a miscellany of discarded household items.

From the stables, she could see the pigs in their field savouring their breakfast slop. She called a good morning to them.

'Yes, best to keep them onside, Daphne,' came a voice behind her. 'Viciously vindictive if one crosses them; just ask poor Moore, nearly took his thumb off a few months ago.'

Charles hobbled over to her, a huge woollen scarf swathed around his neck.

'I knew you'd be first ready – no dilly-dallying with you, Daphne,' Charles chuckled.

'Quite right too. Now I'm perfectly chomping at the bit to have a nosey round this maze of yours, Charles. Spotted it on my way in last night and, believe you me, it took buckets of restraint to not go marching into it immediately.' Daphne had listened to countless tales of Maybridge Castle's maze – it was evidently the feature of the property that tickled Charles the most. He never tired of recounting the story of Isabella Montague, the heiress to a coal fortune who, in 1764, inexplicably ran into the maze at midnight, never to be seen again. And the tale of how, exactly one hundred years later, the same fate befell the daughter of Lord William Sitterton, a famed MP at the time.

'I've a mind to see just what kind of chasm of doom lies at its centre, engulfing any pretty young maiden that crosses it,' Daphne explained. 'Or to thumb my nose at the spectral ghoul intent on dragging young ladies to the underworld. But only, of course, if they're from well-to-do families and partial to solitary midnight strolls in a haunted maze.'

Charles eyed her with a mischievous grin. 'All in good time, Daphne, all in good time. We've the woodland wander first, then a visit to Madame Marla – or perhaps a spot of Tarot cards.'

Daphne emitted an indistinct murmur.

'Now, now, Daphne: I'll none of that cynicism of yours. One has to open one's heart and mind to possibilities – and impossibilities,' Charles gently reprimanded her. 'You and Mrs Thewley are terrible influences upon one another: I'll have to separate the two of you.'

'Having been told countless times that I'm an interfering busybody, it's rather nice to find myself in the company of one who's even more interfering and entirely busier than I,' Daphne replied. 'Whoever would have supposed that I'd find such a kindred spirit?'

They had ambled just beyond the stable now, and Daphne was surprised to find a most intriguing edifice before her. A wrought-iron structure, it appeared to have three chambers, each adjoining the next. The iron appeared rusted and in ill health. Bare tendrils of a creeper clung to the iron, and had made their way to its domed roof. So thick were the tendrils – even despite the absence of foliage – that Daphne couldn't see through the climbers to what lay inside the structure. Daphne could see remnants of paint here and there on the iron columns, a reddish colour which suggested that, at one point in its life, the structure had gleamed colourfully – rather a contrast to its current, shabby state.

Daphne made to approach it, but Charles grabbed her elbow with unexpected force. His voice rang with a sudden sharpness. 'No, you mustn't!'

Puzzled by Charles's impassioned response, Daphne turned to look at him.

'We must keep our distance from the aviary, I'm afraid,' he said, clearing his throat as if to banish the vehemence of a moment ago. 'Some rather gorgeous – and rather rare – finches are nesting in there. Moore is an avid ornithologist, and reliably informs me that, once nesting, these particular finches – the name escapes me now, you'll have to ask him – detest any disturbance whatsoever. Can lead to calamity with the incubation period, some such technical thing. So I must ask you to keep your distance – perhaps in the summer you'll be able to admire the aviary.'

Daphne shrugged. She was far more interested in the maze anyway. Though it did seem a shame that such an elaborate structure was languishing in such disrepair. On the other hand, she reflected, so too was much of the Maybridge Castle environs.

She glanced at her watch. 'Where are all these stragglers? Goodness me, let's go and chivvy them along eh?'

As they turned and walked back past the stables, Daphne could make out Duke prowling around by the front door. Daphne had encountered a number of felines in her years, but never had she met one quite so truly relentless in his outdoor pursuits, clearly having finagled his way out of the castle yet again. He was now diligently sniffing every one of the flagstones, his tail waving purposefully behind him.

'Best keep young master Duke away from those finches, Charles – would hate to think what he might get up to if he sneaks his way into the aviary,' Daphne commented.

Duke greeted them with an abrupt meow, then deigned to allow them to stroke him. It was an act that Charles only achieved with considerable difficulty, his back clearly unhappy with the strain.

Which reminded Daphne: where was his cane? She hadn't seen it since earlier yesterday evening. Since before Winifred Roberts's ... accident. There was no two ways about it: she'd have to broach it with Charles.

'Oh dear, Charles, you all right?' she asked, holding his arm and helping him to straighten back up again. 'Where's that cane of yours? Let me fetch for it before we set off.'

Charles waved his hand dismissively. 'Do you know, I've put it down somewhere and can't for the life of me remember where. This bloody noggin of mine, it's playing all sorts of tricks on me of late. Must start doing those cryptic crosswords again, clear out the cobwebs,' he said, tapping his head.

Daphne narrowed her eyes. This was not the answer she was hoping for. She had wanted Charles to shrug in exaggerated exasperation, tell her off for fussing over him, then send her trotting up to his bedroom where his cane would be leaning against a wardrobe. Then Daphne could inspect the gold handle, conclude happily and swiftly that no, it was not covered in Winifred Roberts's blood, and therefore, no, it had not been put to murderous purpose.

With this response, however, Daphne was left with a nagging suspicion. A suspicion that was growing darker. Could Cousin Charles – kind, generous, slightly dotty

Cousin Charles – really have killed Winifred Roberts? To what end? In the hope that her unfortunate death would send hordes of visitors to his hotel? Salvage his reputation within his family, rescue him from his more-than-precarious financial circumstances? Surely not. But 'surely not' never solved anything. 'Surely not' never led to the truth.

Rather than racing with agility and finesse through Daphne's mind, all this was sluggishly slithering its way into her thoughts. Duke had begun to reach his paws up to her knees, evidently displeased that he appeared to have lost her attention.

'Yes, yes, Duke,' she murmured. 'I can see that you're here.'

She picked him up and turned to see Mrs Thewley emerging from the front door.

'Ah! There he is!' she exclaimed. 'What a conniving little rat you are, Duke, fleeing our chambers and flagrantly demanding attention from poor beleaguered Miss King.'

Daphne handed the squirming cat over to his rightful owner, who tut-tutted dramatically and shook her head at him.

While Mrs Thewley returned Duke to his temporary abode, the other guests finally made their way to the meeting spot outside the castle. Daphne watched as they arrived. Raymond Hammond, bald head sheltered by a tweed flat cap, was blithering affably to his son, who trudged, hands jammed into his pockets, beside him. There was Eleanor Beaumont, removing her leather gloves so that she could show Helena Rackham her glittering wedding ring. Helena was putting on a decent show of being interested, but Daphne suspected that her mind was elsewhere: namely, the newly discovered 'witch burial ground' in the woodland. To her surprise, there too were Mr and Mrs Moore, both as expressionless as Daphne had come to expect.

Surveying them all, Daphne felt herself a child in a particularly tempting sweetshop. Who among them might have had cause to harm Winifred Roberts? What unknown antagonisms lay lurking? Who could Winifred have provoked so much that violence was considered their only recourse? Daphne had to stop herself from rubbing her hands together in glee. Veronica had told her that she was permitted to be intellectually and professionally piqued by murder, but she really ought to stifle the outright jubilation that so often overtook her when getting her teeth into an investigation.

But Veronica wasn't here. And so Daphne allowed herself a certain amount of elation. Imperceptible to the others, of course.

16

The woodland lay at the foot of a small hill behind May-bridge Castle. It was densely populated by oaks that, so Charles explained, had been planted just after the Civil War, to replace those lost in frays. Underfoot, the ground was damp and thick with dead leaves. Daphne had to skip nimbly on occasion to avoid boggy patches, which made maintaining conversations – conversations which needed to yield information and insight – rather challenging.

She could hear Mrs Thewley extolling the virtues of Monet and Renoir to the sullen Kenneth Hammond, who appeared bemused by the old lady and her attentions. Daphne almost giggled when she heard Mrs Thewley off-handedly remark that, 'Of course, flowers and nature are all good and well, but it's an artist's rendering of human flesh that really does set one's pulse racing.'

Daphne had decided to attach herself to the Beau-monts. She wanted to know more about Dr Beaumont's rather fraught demeanour. That he was a troubled man was clear: the faraway look in his eyes, the unbecoming sheen of sweat that he was perpetually beset by. Perhaps he was just an anxious sort. Doctors could, in Daphne's experience, be a rather grumpy lot. Daily decisions about life and death could, she supposed, become somewhat tiring. Could weigh upon a person.

That said, she had gathered that Dr John Beaumont was a general practitioner, so he would be more accustomed to suggesting lozenges and treating ingrown toenails than dicing with death.

He had insisted that she call him by his Christian name, so Daphne began, 'Tell me, John, you must have your fair share of over-wrought and finicking patients? Every GP has an amusing tale or two to tell.'

John gently assisted his wife in avoiding a stagnant puddle, before glancing at Daphne and replying, 'Well, Daphne,' for she too had insisted on dispensing with formalities, 'it's often . . . often rather dull, as it happens. You know, coughs and colds, anxious mothers, elderly people with complaints of tingling legs. Et cetera, et cetera. Nothing that would shock or, I'm sorry to say, amuse you.'

Eleanor Beaumont chimed in, 'Oh he's doing himself down! He loves it, absolutely loves it!'

Daphne looked at John, to see an expression of melancholy flit across his face. He sighed and arranged a smile, patting his wife's hand tenderly. 'I do love what I do, you're right, darling.'

Dr John Beaumont was clearly a man in love. The softness in his face as he spoke to his wife was in sharp contrast with the flinty, exhausted appearance he had presented earlier at breakfast.

'Sometimes, of course, it can be awfully sad,' Eleanor continued. 'There was that young lad last year you saw, the one with what turned out to be gangrene. You spotted that, took one look at that gammy leg, whisked him straight to the hospital. Then that girl a few months ago, the one with – what was it? You saw her right, though, that Macauley girl—'

John cut in abruptly. 'Darling, how many times – please – patient confidentiality! It's – it's *vital* you refrain from sharing my patient's names with perfect strangers!'

Eleanor Beaumont appeared chastened and not a little shocked by her husband's tone and fervour. Tears started to well in her eyes. John's fleeting irritation subsided and he murmured an apology to her, holding her hands tightly.

'I'm sorry, darling, I didn't mean to bark at you like that,' he said. 'And really it's my own silly fault – I shouldn't be telling *you* names. From now on, everyone shall be henceforth known only as Jack or Jill, Humpty or Dumpty, Tweedle-Dee or Tweedle-Dum.'

Eleanor wiped her tears with the handkerchief that she had neglected to return to Mrs Moore, and tentatively smiled at her husband.

'And my apologies to you, Daphne, for framing you as a perfect stranger,' John gave a small bow of deference. 'Because of course we're all getting to know each other very well'

That we are, Daphne thought. That we are.

It was as Daphne was following a frolicking squirrel with her eyes that Mrs Thewley made a declaration that silenced and stilled the group.

'Doctors are a godsend, I don't mind my saying. Back when my husband and my son died, my Dr Mayfield helped me immensely.'

Everyone appeared lost for words. They stood stock still in the woods, looking at Mrs Thewley agape.

Daphne was the first to regain the power of speech. 'Oh, dear Mrs Thewley – I'm so sorry – what a sad, sad thing to have happened,' She took a step towards Mrs Thewley and placed a hand on her arm.

'Thank you, Miss King. Yes it was excessively, obscenely sad. Tuberculosis, both of them,' Mrs Thewley said. 'It was a terrible time, I don't mind admitting. Darkest year of my life, 1901. But here I am to tell the tale, a meddling old dodderer. Duke keeps me young and sprightly, that's what I say.'

The group laughed good-naturedly, with the exception of Mrs Moore. Daphne gazed at the woman. Her habitually imperturbable face was animated with emotion.

She said softly, 'I – we – lost our son that way too. It's an awful disease.'

'My deepest condolences, Mrs Moore,' said Mrs Thewley with sincerity. 'Carry on we must, their memories with us always. Oh dear, what a rather platitudinous thing to say!'

Mrs Moore shook her head quickly, and smiled at Mrs Thewley.

'I say, jolly sorry to be an insensitive so-and-so, and do tell me to bugger off if you'd like to,' Charles said, resting his weight against a tree trunk. 'But here we are at the burial ground. Thought, ah, thought we'd all like to know.'

Daphne glanced about her. Had she been on a solitary wander in the woods, she would not have suspected that here, upon this very spot, the remains of six women had been found. Charles had allowed a group of local history enthusiasts have the run of the forest when he took up residence earlier in the year. They had been convinced, through meticulous research and painstaking cross-referencing of sources, that the site was here. Lo and behold, they had been correct. The news had made a splash in the archaeological community, and, of course in the realms of academia that Helena Rackham had dedicated herself to.

Helena's eyes were wide, an expression of wonder upon her face.

'Golly, this is – gosh – I can't quite – *golly*!' She whipped a notebook from a pocket of her coat and began scribbling in it, her eyes darting around the ground.

Charles chuckled. 'Knew you'd be in your element, Helena!'

'Quite,' she murmured, her tongue sticking out slightly in concentration. 'This is incredible, absolutely incredible. Here, right here, this is earth-shattering in my field, Charles, absolutely earth-shattering.'

Daphne watched as Helena continued to write her notes. If only she had made a discovery that could be deemed earth-shattering. Patience, she told herself. There's time yet to peel back the layers.

17

The room was engulfed in a fug of incense. In the dim light, Daphne looked around at the arcane memorabilia that festooned the walls and the shelves. She had never seen so many beaded items and crystals of uncertain provenance. How Veronica would laugh when she heard about this episode.

Charles had suggested that the group split in two for the next item on the day's itinerary. So it was that Daphne found herself sitting on a cushion at a table with Eleanor Beaumont, John Beaumont and Raymond Hammond, awaiting that most insightful of activities: a Tarot card reading. Mrs Thewley and the others were next door, about to enjoy the wonders of a séance.

When Charles had bought Maybridge Castle and learnt of the many tales of hauntings and unexplained happenings attached to it, he had been delighted. When he also learnt that, just at the edge of the grounds, in a small house on an isolated lane, there lived Madame

Marla and her sister, Madame Thelma, he was positively cock-a-hoop. A haunted castle and two clairvoyants – what better way to lure those partial to Spiritualism?

Daphne cleared her throat. 'Mr Hammond, is this your, ah, maiden voyage into the world of Tarot cards?'

Raymond Hammond smiled sheepishly and took off his tweed flat cap. 'As a matter of fact, Miss King, I'm something of a veteran when it comes to this type of thing.'

'Oooh, me too!' exclaimed Eleanor. 'One of my vices, isn't it, John? I always say, better than spending our money on fashion or mod-cons, gets me out of the house, and I've made so many friends, haven't I, John?'

John nodded, a slight raised eyebrow indicating that he was perhaps not entirely happy with their money being spent on innumerable Tarot card readings.

'What is it that brought you to them, if you don't mind my asking?' Daphne ventured, directing her question at Raymond Hammond. She had spent insufficient time speaking with him, and needed to find more of a footing with him. Her impression of him was of a man with a kindness and sadness at his core.

'I don't mind at all, Miss King,' he began, before explaining that his wife, Kenneth's mother, had died tragically some years ago in a boating accident on Lake Windermere. 'It was when Kenneth was only a small boy, five years old. It was 1919, the war was over, we all felt we could . . . breathe again. Be content again. Enjoy the lives we had – enjoy each other.'

Daphne glanced at the Beaumonts. John squeezed his wife's hand.

'We had decided to indulge in a holiday, get away for a little. My wife and I – her name was Annabel – we had stayed in a quaint little hotel in Lake Windermere just after we were married, so we thought it would rather jolly to go back there. And it was. A lovely little place, oil paintings in the hallways, ceramic ducks on the mantelpiece.'

Raymond appeared lost in a reverie. Daphne wondered how often he had the opportunity to talk about what had happened.

'Oh, apologies, I forget myself,' Raymond said. 'You're not here for a soliloquy, and I suspect our Madame Thelma will be here any moment now. Long and short of it, we wanted to go out on a rowing boat one day. But I – well, I remembered that I needed to place a telegram. Seemed remarkably important at the time.'

'Who was it to?' Eleanor asked. Rather bold, Daphne thought. Bravo.

Raymond paused, blinked. Arranged his features into a semblance of confusion. 'Do you know, I can't recall now. Darned thing, isn't it. Seemed like the be all and end all at the time – now . . . different kettle of fish altogether.

Anyway. I insisted on posting this godforsaken telegram. Kenneth was bored, impatient – as five-year-olds
are wont to be. Annabel, ever the diplomat, suggested
that she take Kenneth out on the boat immediately, and
I would meet them afterwards. After my errand. Well,
twenty minutes or so later I made my way to the lake.
Kenneth – Kenneth was there on the shore, crying. Some
people were looking after him. The fellow hiring out the
boats had gone and got him. By all accounts, it had
become . . . rough, choppy out on the lake. Annabel had
fallen in. They found her later that afternoon.'

John Beaumont was the first to offer a comforting
word, some of his bedside manner evident. Daphne
added, 'That's tragic, Raymond, truly tragic. I'm terribly
sorry for your loss.'

After Mrs Thewley's revelation earlier, Daphne was
now rather of the mind that Maybridge Castle was
something of a magnet for the bereaved and the tragic.

Raymond thanked them, shaking his head and adding,
'There we have it. Lesson to us all. No errand is more
important than the ones we love.'

Daphne thought of Veronica, carousing her way
around New York. She would visit the post office
tomorrow, place a telegram to her hotel.

At that moment, the strings of beads that served as a
door parted theatrically. A woman entered. Madame

Thelma. With a sequinned hat perched upon her head, and an extravagant green kimono wrapped about her person, she cut quite a figure. There was a gash of bright red lipstick upon her mouth, and, as she approached, Daphne noticed that her eyes were glittering with gold. When she spoke, it was with a broad Cumbrian accent somewhat at odds with the mystical glamour that she initially exuded.

'Charlie boy tells me you're here for a little reading? A little peek into what the universe holds for you – what the universe intends for you,' she intoned.

Charlie boy? Daphne would have to ask about that.

'I will allow myself to be guided as to who shall receive the gift of a reading first,' Madame Thelma sat gracefully on one of the cushioned chairs around the table. She closed her eyes and took a deep breath. 'You.'

Daphne looked at the finger pointing at her and had to exert rather a lot of effort to abstain from rolling her eyes.

'Very well,' she assented, placing one hand on top of the other. 'Curious to hear what the old universe wants to say to me. Postcard might be easier.'

Madame Thelma narrowed her eyes. 'I see. An unbeliever. Well, no matter. Let us begin.'

With that, she laid out in front of her the stack of cards and began to shuffle them with laboured ceremony.

Madame Thelma turned over the first card. 'Queen of

Swords. This speaks of perceptiveness. Clear-sightedness. You see the world around you as it really is; for what it really is.'

Daphne made a sound of approval.

Another card was turned over. 'Seven of Pentacles. This tells me of your diligence, you work hard. And your hard work yields rewards.'

Daphne could get used to this. Perhaps she had been too quick to judge Spiritualism and its pursuits.

'The reversed Eight of Swords,' Madame Thelma announced. 'Have you recently been ... imprisoning yourself? Containing yourself, or forbidding yourself from ... being your true self?'

Daphne frowned.

'The reversed Eight of Swords implores you to strive for self-acceptance. Liberate yourself from any shackles weighing you down. Freedom lies ahead if you are willing to embrace it.' A note of encouragement had appeared in Madame Thelma's voice.

'Now .... you.' Madame Thelma pointed at John Beaumont. He smiled and smoothed out his moustache.

'First ...' the woman's hand hovered over the card before she turned it. 'Ah. The Lovers!'

Eleanor giggled and leant her head against John's shoulder momentarily.

Madame Thelma continued, 'Unity, partnership. Love!'

Waggling her left hand, Eleanor exclaimed, 'We're still practically newly-weds! He's my hubby, you see, tied the knot in August. Unity and partnership and love is spot-on!'

Madame Thelma smiled tolerantly. 'The next card is . . . the star card.'

She explained that this spoke of healing and caring. Eleanor emitted a squeal.

'He's only a bleeding doctor! A doctor! All he does all day every day is heal and care for people! Oh Madame Thelma, you are by far – by *far* – the best I've seen. Absolutely top notch. Wait 'til I tell Barbara and the girls about this. Charles'll be booked out 'til next Christmas!'

Madame Thelma did not appear to be listening. She had turned over the final card and was staring at it. She displayed it to John. It showed a man carrying – struggling to carry – a collection of swords.

'The Seven of Swords reversed,' Madame Thelma declared, frowning. 'It speaks of holding a secret. A secret which weighs heavily upon you. Which burdens you.'

John Beaumont's eyes had grown cold. He glared at Madame Thelma.

'Such an encumbrance must be shed if you are to thrive. You must rid yourself of this burden. Only by sharing your secret can you go on.'

Eleanor Beaumont did not giggle this time. Nor did she rest her head against her husband's shoulder.

'Oh,' she said. 'Oh, that's a . . . that doesn't sound right. Me and my hubby, we don't keep any secrets, do we, John?' She looked at him, searching for reassurance.

Daphne watched as he gathered his composure and cleared his throat. 'Well, I suppose there is that terrible secret I've been keeping from you.'

Eleanor turned pale.

'It's a struggle to admit it, but here goes.' He took a deep breath. 'I really, really, *really* . . . dislike the pea soup that your mother makes for us when we visit. Very much indeed.'

Eleanor let out an exhalation and flicked her husband's arm. 'Ohhh, John! You are a one!'

Daphne eyed the doctor levelly. He certainly was a one. And one that she might have to pry a little more into.

18

Meanwhile, in the room next door, Mrs Thewley and her eagle eyes were presiding over a séance with Madame Marla. She knew that she had to calibrate her observational powers to their highest, adjust her levels of scrutiny to hitherto unknown levels. She knew that she must not allow any details to go unnoticed, any titbits of information to be lost. She knew that she could not let Miss King down.

As she would relay to Daphne later that evening, the séance had begun as all séances, in her experience, did.

After the group – herself, Charles, Helena Rackham and Kenneth Hammond – had arranged themselves around the table, the flamboyant Madame Marla had floated into the room. Her hands were heavily beringed, stones all of colours, shapes and sizes adorning her fingers. Her dress was black, cuffed by a gold fringe which matched the bangles clanking heavily against the table when she moved her arms.

'Before we begin, Madame Marla,' Charles announced. 'May I introduce to you Mrs Amelia Thewley, chief sceptic and rampaging debunker.'

Madame Marla raised her eyebrows and looked at Mrs Thewley.

'Aha. What an honour, Mrs Thewley,' she rejoined playfully. 'Your name is very well known in our circles. Very well known indeed. What a pity those women in the Margate grotto weren't terribly clued up. Clearly not up to date with their subscription to *Spiritualism Now*.'

Mrs Thewley smirked light-heartedly. Yes, she was very familiar with that particular publication. Circulated monthly among those of a Spiritualist bent, it featured stories of eventful séances, tales of ghost-hunters – and had, just two months ago, seen fit to interview Mrs Amelia Thewley. She had always shied away from the spotlight, had always declined requests for 'little chats' with those in the Spiritualist community who showed an interest in her. Lone wolf, is how she preferred to think of herself. Striding intently and unwaveringly towards the truth. But her latent narcissism had made her accept when that nice young man from *Spiritualism Now* had turned up on her doorstep. He had flattered her and wheedled her, and, hang it – she was far too old to look a gift horse in the mouth. Particularly a very handsome gift horse who took three hours out of his day to listen to her rambling, stroke Duke and drink milky tea. She had, however, wondered whether such an exercise would, at some point, compromise her ability to sneak into séances and the like undetected.

Madame Marla still had her gaze fixed on Mrs Thewley.

'Let us see whether we have any visitors today who might want a word or two with you, Mrs Thewley.'

The room was then plunged into darkness, Madame Marla having extinguished all but one of the candles. It now flickered and danced, illuminating the angles and crevices of the attendees' faces – making them look like Caravaggio had rendered them, Mrs Thewley observed.

Mrs Thewley always enjoyed this part. The anticipation, the hush. Even as a staunch unbeliever, she always found herself swept along by the pomp and the grandeur. The ritual of it, the almost atavistic nature of sitting in the dark, in a circle, wishing to commune with the spirits. Of course, she thought it all utter hogwash. But that didn't mean she couldn't appreciate the spectacle of it. Soon, she reflected, would come the wobbling of the table, the knocks. Madame Marla would affect some peculiar intonations or other, hurl out some vague proclamations that would strike a nerve with someone present – someone suggestible. Madame Marla would already have sized up the participants, fixed upon her prey. Which of them looked the most easily led? Which the most likely to seize upon bombastic utterances flung about?

It took only minutes for Mrs Thewley to see that Madame Marla had pinpointed precisely the victim she herself would have chosen from the assorted guests.

'There . . . there appears to be someone here . . .' Madame Marla moaned, her eyelids fluttering rapidly. Her voice was deeper than it had been when she sat down, a husky texture to it that, Mrs Thewley supposed, mediums imagined to convey gravity.

'Hello? Hello? If you're here . . .'

A knock to the wall.

Mrs Thewley sighed. Here we go, she thought.

'Yes . . . she's here . . . it's a woman,' Madame Marla continued. The guests had been instructed to hold hands, and Mrs Thewley was finding that young Kenneth Hammond possessed quite the slippery grip.

'She says . . .'

Does she say I'd like 20 per cent of whatever Charles has coughed up for this song and dance? Mrs Thewley thought ungenerously.

'She says that – that – she's – sorry,' Madame Marla stuttered. 'She says . . . she says she – wanted to tell you in person . . . but it was too late.'

Mrs Thewley's eyes travelled around, searching eve-ryone in the room with a quick, practised glance. Charles was looking bemused, Kenneth Hammond a little bored. Helena Rackham, however, looked to be perched on the edge of her seat, mesmerised by the ramblings.

'She – seeks forgiveness from beyond the grave.'

Why could they never just seek a nice cup of tea from beyond the grave? Mrs Thewley wondered. Always for-giveness, or redemption, or answers. It always became quite dull at this point. For who among us has never sinned against another? Allowed a grudge to take hold and remain rooted in place? We all, at some point or another, have committed ills – however slight, however unintentional – against others. All it took was a few well-judged turns of the screw, and someone would always start howling and wailing about wanting to change, or having already changed.

Madame Marla paused, scanned the table, the shadows dancing upon everyone's faces. 'She wants me . . . wants me to say . . . sorry to . . . Ratty?'

A sharp gasp.

Helena Rackham leapt from her chair, staggered back-wards from the table. 'Ratty?' she repeated.

Madame Marla nodded slowly.

Helena's eyes darted around the room, twiddling a

strand of her faded blonde hair as she did. 'That – that's . . .' she began. 'Please excuse me, I find myself in need of some fresh air.'

Charles unsteadily stood as she left, Kenneth also rose politely. Mrs Thewley watched as Helena hastily charged out of the room.

Adieu, Ratty, Mrs Thewley thought to herself. Miss King will be immensely interested to hear about this.

19

Daphne was perched on the stone wall outside the clairvoyant sisters' house when Helena Rackham tore through the front door, gulping for air.

'I say, Helena.' She came towards her and placed a hand on her back. 'You look like you've seen a ghost.' Too late, Daphne realised the misfortune of this turn of phrase.

'I – I – it was terribly stuffy in there,' Helena spluttered. 'Couldn't . . . c-couldn't quite catch my breath.'

Daphne could sympathise. 'There was rather a lot of that incense floating around, wasn't there? Thought I might have had a migraine coming on. Had to step out too after we all had our readings.'

Helena appeared to be calming down, her breath slowing to a regular pace. 'Don't know why I let Charles persuade me to come to this – I'd far rather be scribbling in my notebook.'

'You and I both, Helena,' Daphne remarked. 'I don't go in for all this Spiritualist claptrap, if I'm to be honest.'

At this, Helena's panic rose again. 'Well, no, neither did I – but then – but, well . . .'

Well, well. Daphne thought. Something appears to have happened at the séance. She could only hope that Mrs Thewley had applied her acumen to the situation and would be able to relay all to her later. Unless Helena Rackham could be prevailed upon to spill the beans now.

'What is it, Helena?' Daphne affected her most concerned voice.

'Oh . . . nothing, nothing,' Helena shook her head. 'Just – well, one never knows, does one.'

Daphne snorted unintentionally. One certainly never did know.

The others came out of the house, blinking and squinting now that they were back in daylight.

'What-ho, Daphne!' shouted Charles. 'Enjoy yourself in there?'

Daphne said that she really rather had enjoyed herself, yes.

'Seen Mr and Mrs Moore about anywhere?' Charles continued. 'They had a few errands to run in the village, but I understood that they'd be back by n— Oh, speak of the devil!'

Mr and Mrs Moore marched towards the house, a parcel under Mr Moore's arm and a paper bag of what appeared to be carrots in Mrs Moore's hand.

'Right-o,' Charles proclaimed, clapping his hands together. 'I say we amble our way back to Maybridge. It's what, one o'clock now? A light lunch, courtesy of Mrs Moore, before a spot of free time and then our evening commences?'

There was a collective nod, but Daphne raised her hand tentatively as if offering an answer to an algebra conundrum that she hadn't quite finished working out.

'I'm rather one for missing my lunch, generally.' It was a lie, a terrible lie that Daphne regretted almost instantly. She was a creature of habit, and her habit was to have lunch at precisely one thirty every day, by hook or by crook, come rain or shine. On the odd occasion that circumstances had detained her from this routine, she had become incrementally snappier, more irrational and more prone to outbursts of sarcasm with every minute that passed. It was a risk, granted. But she needed some time away from the group. Distance would yield clarity. Even if that perspicacity was accompanied by hunger and rage.

'I quite fancy taking myself on a little exploration,' she explained.

'Are you quite sure, Daphne?' Charles asked. 'I'd hate for you to miss out on the lavish and rather macabre feast that Mrs Moore is laying on for us: devilled eggs, tongue sandwiches, all swilled down with mulled wine.

I know it's only lunchtime, but I rather thought that goblets of crimson nectar might be just the ticket after our traipsing out here in the cold.'

Daphne hesitated. Devilled eggs were one of her favourites. The tongue sandwich she could leave. And mulled wine would certainly have a pleasingly soothing effect.

No, Daphne, she told herself. Now is not the time for anything pleasing or soothing. Now is the time to keep one's senses alert and one's mind sharp.

'I've a hankering for stretching my legs, making the acquaintance of any souls that I might meet while they're wandering between here and the hereafter,' she insisted amiably.

'Well, naturally, Daphne,' Charles replied. 'I should expect nothing less from you. Cousin Veronica simply adores telling us all about your solitary walks during which you invariably crack the most devilish of cases or experience a sudden epiphany the likes of which even Archimedes would covet.'

John Beaumont had been listening intently, and shifted on his feet. 'Well that rather implies that Daphne here is grappling with some kind of mystery. Is that the case?'

Daphne looked at him squarely. 'For a woman in my line of work, John, the world has a surfeit of mysteries.

Always one creature or another holding some secrets, wouldn't you agree?'

John could not hold her stare, but rather turned to his wife and announced that the only mystery he was interested in solving was the mystery of just how many devilled eggs he'd manage to eat during lunch back at Maybridge Castle. To which Eleanor tittered, flicked him on the arm once more and repeated her earlier proclamation that he really was a one.

As the group began to head back towards the castle, Mrs Thewley hung back for a moment and offered her now customary wink to Daphne. 'Now, duckie, I don't wish to tantalise you to no good end – but I suspect you'll be rather interested in what I have to tell you about our séance.'

Daphne whispered confidentially, 'Yes, I should quite like to know what exactly sent Helena Rackham charging out of there.'

'All in good time, Miss King,' Mrs Thewley winked again. 'Duke and I will be waiting in our chambers at, say, eleven again?'

Crikey, Daphne thought. What on earth would Veronica say if she knew that Daphne was being invited to the chambers of another woman? She smiled. What indeed.

Mrs Thewley tottered after the others with surprising speed, and Daphne gathered her thoughts. The blue sky of the morning had become overcast, and she felt a splash of rain. Not the perfect conditions for one of her epiphanic strolls. If she were caught in a downpour *and* she was hungry, she could only imagine the pit of despair into which she would be hurled. There had been a terrible episode back in May, when she and Veronica had gone to New York for the first time. Veronica had insisted on a turn around Central Park, just as the hour had struck one. Daphne knew it was dangerous ground, that there was but thirty minutes until she would require – nay, need – sustenance. But she had acquiesced. And catastrophe had ensued. No, she wasn't interested in that statue, nor was she particularly keen to investigate those pine cones. And no, she certainly couldn't give a fig for stopping and discussing the state of modern drama with some particularly over-familiar Broadway friends that Veronica had made. Then, to cap it all, the rain had started. When they returned to their hotel room, Daphne – drenched and ravenous – had, to her eternal shame and embarrassment, launched into what could only be termed a tantrum.

So she had learnt her lesson: rain and hunger were two elements that should never, under any circumstances, be mixed.

The chapel. That was it. She knew there was a chapel somewhere in the woods. Peaceful, sheltered solitude was what she needed now. So to the chapel she went.

20

The bogs dotted throughout the woodland had been difficult to avoid, but avoid them she had. The chapel was small; from the outside it looked barely bigger than the derelict yet sacrosanct aviary back at Maybridge Castle. The ancient-looking wooden door creaked as she heaved it open, and once she stepped inside, the temperature dropped perceptibly.

There were perhaps ten pews in the chapel, of the sort that looked designed to promote discomfort. The backs were set at a stiff ninety degree angle to the seat, and Daphne couldn't even see any of the embroidered cushions that she knew were usually supplied to ease the knees of the kneeling congregants. Her boots click-clacked on the stone floor as she approached one of the pews.

The altar was bare, no adornment or fripperies visible. The only feature that strayed from the austere was a single stained-glass pane above an alcove to the left of the altar. Daphne peered up at it, though now that the afternoon had taken a turn towards the dismal, it was difficult to make out the scene in the glass with no sunlight to illuminate it. It was, she concluded, Jesus raising Lazarus from the dead. Very much in keeping with the preternatural goings-on that seemed to define Maybridge Castle and its surroundings.

She sat in one of the pews, listened to the rain pelting down on the chapel's slate roof. Winifred Roberts had died, that much was certain. The local police had concluded it – far too swiftly for Daphne's liking – an accident. No questions for anyone present, no further visit to seek any clarification on the events leading up to and following the discovery of Winifred's body. Daphne knew it was no accident. She had learnt over the last year to listen to that nagging voice that piped up to tell her that something was amiss. Her instincts had rarely failed her. Come to think of it: her instincts had *never* failed her. Winifred Roberts had been struck, been pushed down those stairs. And Daphne's instincts told her it had been at the hand of someone present in their group. The possibility of an external agent had, of course, crossed her mind. Someone, feasibly, could have snuck into the house while it was shrouded in silence and darkness during their little game. But there was something queer about the atmosphere, something off about the dynamic in the group of guests that persuaded Daphne it had to be one of them.

Then, of course, she found herself circling the notion that Charles might have been driven to do something rash. Driven by desperation and foolishness to carry out an act of violence so as to avoid ignominy and ridicule. She could not rule him out, but by God did she wish she could.

Raymond Hammond and his son Kenneth, the tragic sadness that defined and permeated their lives. Winifred Roberts had been, as far as Daphne could tell, mocking them cruelly at the drinks yesterday evening. From what she had seen so far of Kenneth Hammond, he seemed every bit an angry young man. Raymond, however . . . Raymond appeared harmless. Sad, yes. Destined to for ever mourn his wife and regret the decisions he made in the hour or so before her death? Quite probably. But capable of battering a woman on the head all because of a callous comment and a few unthinking jibes? Surely not. Ugh, there it was again, rearing its ugly head: the deadening 'surely not'. She must endeavour to jettison that from her thought processes.

Helena Rackham appeared a jittery specimen. What was that charge that had passed through the room when she and Winifred had been introduced to one another? Or had Daphne merely imagined it? Could it simply be that Helena was . . . the type to be possessed of a charge when introduced to a rather glamorous, some would argue attractive woman? It didn't quite fit, Daphne decided. Once she had learnt of the happenings during the séance, she might be better positioned to hypothesise about the nervy Helena Rackham. Perhaps reading her work might shed some light on the woman behind the anxious teeth-tapping and the golly-goshing.

Daphne sighed. There was a hefty amount of work to be done. And she hadn't even begun ruminating about the Beaumonts. Eleanor, with her giggling and her guileless happiness. She was clearly smitten with her husband. He, on the other hand, now *he* was someone to keep her eye on. Dr John Beaumont, who seemed to be labouring under the weight of the world. Dr John Beaumont, tender towards his doting wife, passionate about his profession. Sweaty of brow, intense of expression, Dr John Beaumont. Then there was the matter of the Tarot cards. Of course, Daphne knew that the cards themselves held no water. It was all so much hogwash and tripe. But it was the reaction that was key. What was it that Madame Marla had said? Burdened by a secret. If Dr John Beaumont's one secret was his dislike for his mother-in-law's pea soup, then Daphne would jolly well eat her hat. No, he was hiding something.

There were the Moores, of course. The Moores should

be held in just the same regard as the hotel guests. She couldn't quite get a handle on them, however. She wondered whether, in fact, she might not be told by a forthcoming villager that, yes, the Moores were wonderful people – shame they died fifty years ago in a tragic fire, and that yes, rumour does have it that they still stalk the corridors of Maybridge Castle, tending to the needs of whoever the current resident might be.

Daphne chuckled to herself. Spectral domestic staff indeed. She had only been in Maybridge Castle for one night and already it was affecting her ability to think rationally. She could see why it had the reputation that it did.

'Ahem, ah, hallo,' came a voice. Daphne looked towards the altar and saw a vicar standing, hands clasped behind his back. He smiled warmly at her, and bowed his head slightly. His thick, curly hair hung loosely about his rather large ears. He wore circular spectacles which, even from a distance of three pews, Daphne could see had exceptionally thick lenses. These rendered his eyes tiny blue dots, which nevertheless glinted curiously at her.

She stood and stepped towards him. 'Hello, do excuse me. I was in need of respite from the weather – and some solitude.'

The vicar shook her hand firmly. Up close, he was

shorter than she had imagined, barely reaching Daphne's shoulders. 'Respite from the world, that's what we offer – and, conversely, the opportunity to re-establish one's ties with said world. I'm the Reverend Mr St John Smith, and I shan't trespass upon your solitude, so please do continue in your contemplations.'

Daphne introduced herself, explaining that she was a guest at Maybridge Castle. 'And I was getting myself tied up in all sorts of solitary knots, so please do stay.'

An outside perspective on Maybridge Castle could be just the ticket at this juncture.

'Tell me, Mr Smith, how long have you been … stationed here in Asperdale?' she asked. 'Cousin Charles has thoroughly enjoyed his months here – I do hope he's not been causing too much of a stir amongst the locals. Or if he has been, I hope it's been a deliciously enjoyable stir – not one of those terribly irksome stirs.'

The vicar smiled. 'This is my – let me think – twelfth year here in Asperdale. It's a quiet place, I'll grant you, and your cousin Charles's arrival did set quite a few tongues wagging.'

Daphne thought fleetingly of clarifying that Charles was not, in fact, her direct cousin, but Veronica's – however this interjection would, perhaps, be overly complicated and might only serve to delay the offering of any insightful nuggets this man of the cloth might have.

'He's, as I'm sure you know, a rather extravagant fellow. Given to . . . flights of fancy, shall we say? But he knows how to endear himself to people, which is quite the gift. He's truly won over the villagers now,' the vicar explained, a smile upon his face.

'Well, I'm glad to hear he has his feet under the table – that sounds about right,' Daphne remarked.

'Once that unfortunate business was all over with, of course,' Mr Smith added matter-of-factly.

If Daphne didn't know better, she would have said that, at that very moment, her ears physically and visibly pricked up. If there was an unfortunate business to unpick, then Daphne King would do just that.

'Oh yes, we heard about that. Ghastly, really, wasn't it?' Daphne replied.

'Yes, the young man was something of a ne'er-do-well, set his sights on your cousin Charles and his good nature, so I understand. Thank goodness trusty old Mrs Moore was on hand to call a spade a spade. Not one to have the wool pulled over her eyes, Mrs Moore,' the vicar went on. He really was a talkative one, Daphne thought.

'Oh heavens, yes,' Daphne agreed. 'Oh – apologies – is that rather . . . an indelicate phrasing?'

'Invoking the firmament is quite acceptable in this day and age; I like to think myself a modern representative of the Church,' Mr Smith reassured her.

'In any case, we couldn't believe it when we heard what that young man – what was his name again? – had done,' Daphne said. She, of course, hadn't the foggiest what this young man had done, and certainly had no idea what his name was. But something had told her that there was more to be gained from adopting the role of outraged rather than ignorant relation.

'Jim Sullivan, that was his name. Or at least that's what he *said* his name was. Set the whole village talking, naturally, this rogue thieving from under your cousin's nose, masquerading as a gardener. Which was an inconvenient profession to choose, given all his allergies. As I say, I knew him quite well, but he pulled the wool over my eyes. It was all down to Mrs Moore's ingenuity and instincts that it was brought to light. After which, your cousin was extremely lenient on the boy – told him to leave, but didn't alert the police to his criminal ways,' Mr Smith explained. 'A good Christian man, your cousin.'

So a young man had been stealing from Charles. A young man who had, she presumed, been living in the grounds and acting as a gardener. And who'd been told to sling his hook after Mrs Moore delivered intelligence to Charles about the man's underhand dealings. The plot was thickening. Things certainly were starting to slant and shift.

'And what became of this Jim Sullivan, after his crooked ways were uncovered?' Daphne probed.

Mr Smith flapped his hands noncommittally. 'Heaven only knows. I did speak with him, try to talk some inclination for repentance into him. But he was a stubborn boy, no remorse about his actions. This was, oh, May it all happened. Some from the village say they've seen him gadding about here and there – but I haven't set eyes on him since your cousin sent him on his way.'

As he spoke, the vicar had been diligently polishing a silver chalice. He puffed his breath on to it once more before placing it upon the altar.

'A shame for all involved, truly it was. Your uncle has such a trusting nature – I do believe that this incident shook him somewhat,' he concluded.

Why hadn't Charles mentioned any of this to Veronica? Had he been embarrassed? That he'd employed a young man who had gone on to take advantage of his kind-heartedness, his natural belief in the good of everyone? It was possible. If Charles had thrown Jim Sullivan out, who knew what vengeful impulses the boy might harbour. Could he have snuck into the house last night, bludgeoned Winifred out of … what? Malice against Charles? That didn't quite make sense. Yet. Kill someone in Charles's house to … sabotage him? Give Maybridge Castle a reputation for bloodshed and menace? That was at odds with her countering theory about why Charles himself might have carried out the deed.

'As I say, nasty business,' Mr Smith was continuing. 'In any case: all in the past now. One must look to the future, don't you agree?'

'I'm afraid I don't quite agree, Mr Smith,' Daphne contended, glancing up at the stained-glass window. 'My own opinion – formed through experience of one sort or another, you understand – is that it's rather difficult to keep the past dead and buried. Rather more difficult than most of us would like to admit.'

21

It was only a quarter to two. Mr Smith had left her to her solitude so that he could conduct his weekly inventory of the communion wine (naming no names, he'd told her, he had his theories about why he was having to restock the supplies quite so frequently). Daphne could foresee the scene that would meet her were she to return to Maybridge Castle so soon after bidding adieu to the others. They would be assembled around the dining table, politely discussing the morning's events. Some would be dismissing the séance, the Tarot cards – a diverting lot of bunkum. Others, the more delicate among them, would be silently considering whether it really had been entirely tommy-rot. Had there been nods towards a hitherto undisclosed truth? Were there nuances in the Tarot cards that hinted at a foible that had long been avoided? There would be tension, undoubtedly. Mrs Thewley would be doing her utmost to winkle truths and disclosures out of her fellow guests, as, of course, would Daphne. Somehow the thought of it all exhausted her. She had two more days and nights at Maybridge Castle. That was an unthinkable number of hours to spend vigilantly keeping watch over the guests, their interactions and their habits. This was, after all, supposed to be Daphne's holiday. A few days away from the business of crime and its machinations.

Pull yourself together, Daphne, she chastised herself. This was her job – more than her job, this was her vocation. It had been a year of honing her craft, of learning how to finesse the skills she already possessed. Before that, when by day she was the *Chronicle*'s resident agony columnist, she had day-dreamed about being a crime reporter. Following her nose, inveigling her way into networks of informers, victims and perpetrators. Gaining the trust of the voiceless, cajoling the malefactors into gloating about their deeds.

This was what she, Daphne King, did. It was her *raison d'être*, her driving force. Whenever despondency poured poison into her ear, Veronica would grip her by the shoulders and remind her of all this. Veronica was proud of her. Granted, the odd hours that Daphne sometimes needed to keep, and the nights spent jotting endlessly in her notebooks did occasionally grate on Veronica. But, all things considered, she was utterly supportive of Daphne's calling.

And if ever there was a time to knuckle down, pull her socks up and bloody well get on with it – it was now, when something was amiss in the house of Veronica's own cousin.

She glanced out of the window and could see that the rain had subsided. No excuse. Buttoning her coat back up, Daphne heaved open the chapel door. Back to May-bridge Castle it was.

22

After trudging through the woodland, tipping her head at the witch burial ground in respect, she made her way back around to the front of the castle and rang the doorbell. She was met by Mr Moore who, to her utter surprise, was . . . smiling at her rather warmly.

'Miss King,' he said, a slight but notable lilt in his voice which, to her mind, denoted pleasure at seeing her. 'We were wondering where you'd got to. Please – come in.'

'Why thank you, Mr Moore,' Daphne replied, easing her arms out of her coat as Moore took it from her. 'Yes, I rather lost myself in the woods, met the Reverend Mr Smith . . .'

A snort from Mr Moore. 'Oh yes, Mr Smith – a man with an awful lot to say for himself. Most of which is best digested with a rather large pinch of salt.'

Daphne was, to put it mildly, puzzled. Was Moore drunk? Had he and Mrs Moore been finishing off some of the sherry in between carrying out their errands that afternoon? She had never heard the man speak so freely, engage so animatedly with . . . anyone.

'Yes, seemed like an interesting chap,' she said while she made her way along the entrance hallway, back to the drawing room. 'Speaks very highly of Mrs Moore, I must say.'

Moore was a man whose back was, it seemed to Daphne, held a ram-rod straight posture at all times. At this comment, however, he seemed to draw himself up even more, adding at least an inch to his height.

'People who know Mrs Moore do tend to speak highly of her,' he replied. 'If I may say so.'

Now here was a side to Moore that she would not have suspected lay dormant underneath his ostensibly humourless exterior. A man who took pride in his wife. Who, if not beamed, then at the very least gave the hint that, were he free to, were the terms of his employment less restrictive, he would indeed be beaming now. Possibly even skipping.

Daphne looked at him in curiosity. 'They're all in there, I suppose?' she asked, nodding towards the drawing room.

'Indeed they are, Miss King,' Moore replied. 'Lunch finished rather quickly, seems everyone was ravenous. No standing on ceremony over devilled eggs that Mrs Moore served up. Extremely delicious, even if I do say so myself.

Daphne opened the door to a most unexpected scene. Laughter was ringing throughout the room, the guests united in a mirth that had heretofore been only strained at.

'My dear Mrs Thewley,' Raymond Hammond was saying in between chuckles, 'you must be pulling our legs, no?'

'Oh I assure you, Mr Hammond,' the old woman replied. 'It all happened *precisely* as I outlined, *precisely*. Duke can verify it, can't you, Duke?'

The cat was stretched beside Mrs Thewley on the sofa, his head lolling off the cushion at an alarming angle. His legs were elongated and, lying on his back, a white patch on his tummy was exposed.

'Crikey,' Daphne said as she stood in the doorway, hands in pockets, not hiding the bemusement on her face. 'What's all this?'

Kenneth Hammond, surly, sullen, sulking Kenneth Hammond proffered an answer. 'It's Mrs Thewley – she's been positively scandalising us with wicked tales.'

'Kenneth, you fool nobody by pretending that you haven't heard far, far worse at public houses in Cambridge after your lectures,' Mrs Thewley retorted, grinning. 'If indeed you young things ever make it to such trifles as lectures.'

Daphne marvelled at Mrs Thewley. While she had been sitting in a cold, damp chapel, attempting to draw things into shape, Mrs Thewley had been here – drawing the assorted players into her own charismatic orbit.

'Now, Miss King, I've a proposal for you,' Mrs Thewley went on. 'Mr Moore has shared the most splendid piece of news.'

Mr Moore had evidently been in gregarious form all afternoon.

Helena Rackham chimed in, 'Yes, do listen, Daphne. Mrs Thewley has been trying to recruit some of us, but we think you'd appreciate this far more than us.'

Now Daphne was intrigued.

'According to Mr Moore, there's the most wonderful antiques emporium just a stone's throw away,' Mrs Thewley explained. 'Sheep in a Bucket is the name of the establishment. Now, just as Mrs Beaumont here', she nodded towards Eleanor, 'has her vice of Tarot cards and the like, I too have my vice: the never-ending search for and acquisition of cat-based ornaments.'

Daphne spluttered in disbelief and exchanged a glance with Charles.

'Yes, one wouldn't expect such an … interesting inclination from one as cultured and worldly as Mrs Thewley,' Charles contributed. 'But, having heard her speechify on the subject, I'm half-convinced of the merits of a few porcelain tabbies knocking about the place.'

Mrs Thewley tsked. 'No need to mock, Charles. One

can neither choose nor curtail one's own predilections. Now, it's been decided, Miss King, that you're to escort me to the aforementioned shop.'

'Well that sounds like a fun expedition,' Daphne replied. 'Tomorrow after breakfast?'

'Oh don't be silly, duckie.' Mrs Thewley tsked again. 'When one hears of an antiques emporium, one visits it immediately. What would happen if I were to rest on my laurels, trot down there tomorrow and make enquiries about porcelain cats, only to be told, yes Madam, we had a wonderful assortment, but a gentleman whisked them all off to his pied-à-terre just yesterday, in fact? I ask you, Miss King, would you be able to live with yourself if you were responsible for such calamitous dithering?'

Daphne looked at her ruefully. What the devil was she playing at? Both of them absent themselves from the castle? Nobody here to observe, to pore over information, to study the comings and goings of the guests – of the *suspects*. Daphne thought for a moment. She had known Mrs Thewley for less than twenty-four hours. But what she knew, she trusted.

'Well, I had better get my coat back on then, hadn't I?' she replied.

23

The day's occurrences were proceeding from the outlandish – séances, Tarot cards, witch burial grounds – to the positively ludicrous.

'Are you sure this is safe, Charles?' Daphne asked, looking at the vehicle that sat before her.

Charles laughed heartily. 'Cross my heart, hope to die,' he proclaimed, swooping a hand across his chest.

She had not seen it earlier in her survey of the stables, too distracted was she by the haphazard nature of their contents. But here it was now, hidden behind a wooden pallet at the back of the main stable. A pristine, gleaming motorcycle – with sidecar.

The saddle was a cream leather colour, while the motorcycle itself was a dark brown. As she circled it, Charles was listing its specifications: its horsepower (was it 750 cc? Daphne couldn't be sure), its mileage (somewhere in the region of 15,000 miles. Whether that was good or bad, Daphne had no idea), its provenance (lovely chap in Edinburgh, offloading it because he had a terrible case of restless leg syndrome, could no longer trust himself on it).

While Daphne was dubious, Mrs Thewley made no attempt to conceal her excitement. 'Miss King, I have lived an eventful life. One of colour and intrigue. But never, *never* have I ridden in the sidecar of such a beautiful machine. If you refuse to grant me this wish, I'm afraid that I will consider our budding friendship – promising though it may be – dead in the water,' she declared, cradling a slumbering Duke in her arms. 'Of course, Duke and I shall *both* be enjoying our jaunt.'

Charles assured Daphne once again that the motorcycle was perfectly roadworthy and reliable, although he did urge her to return within the hour, for it would soon be dusk, and the motorcycle's lights did not always take kindly to being switched on.

'Very well,' Daphne answered. 'Far be it from me to deny Mrs Thewley this wish. Remind me of the route, Charles?'

Charles explained once more that it really was a very straightforward route (end of the driveway, turn right, keep going, then turn left at the horseshoe affixed to the pole), and then he went to a cupboard next to the motorcycle. Its doors were hanging off precariously and he winced in pain as a nail jabbed his hand. He rummaged for a few moments before turning around, brandishing two black helmets and one pair of goggles.

'Bagsy those goggles!' Mrs Thewley exclaimed. 'I'd hate to get a speck of dust in my eye, that would ruin my trip entirely.'

Daphne found herself laughing uncontrollably. She looked up to find that Mr Moore, who had accompanied them to the stables, had also taken leave of his self-control and was laughing at the scene.

Once again, she was struck by the warming notion of telling Veronica all about these escapades. Was she really about to load an elderly lady and her cat into a motor-cycle's sidecar, before hurtling off down a country land on a quest to purchase porcelain felines? Yes, it would appear that she very much was.

She helped Mrs Thewley into the sidecar. Mrs Thewley nimbly folded her legs beneath her and held out her hands expectantly. Charles delivered Duke into her arms.

'Now, Duke, there's to be none of your silliness, you hear?' she said. 'Miss King is doing us a tremendous favour, and we are both of us to be on our *best* behaviour.' She looked up at Daphne. 'Duke has promised that he'll neither yowl nor howl nor scratch nor hiss. He understands the seriousness of our current situation, and will do all he can to ensure that a pleasurable outing is had by all.'

'That's very heartening, thank you, Duke.' Daphne lifted one of his paws and shook it. She positioned the helmet upon her head and tightened the clasp. Mr Moore was wheeling the motorcycle – complete with populated sidecar – out of the stable, and Charles was wittering on about it being a shame he hadn't fixed his camera: this would be a sterling scene to capture for posterity.

Daphne followed the motorcycle out into the gravel driveway and took a deep breath. 'Well, here goes nothing, Charles!' she announced as she hoisted one leg over the saddle.

'If you meet your maker on this journey, I do swear to tell Veronica that you went out in a blaze of glory, and that you looked ever so fetching in your helmet,' Charles said, saluting her.

And with that, she kick-started the motorcycle and was on her way.

To say that she was a cautious driver would be a misleading statement.

'For the love of all that is holy, Miss King,' shouted Mrs Thewley over the drone of the engine, 'will you please pick up the pace? I'll have passed into the great unknown by the time we get there at this rate.'

Daphne kept her eyes on the road. 'Please don't distract me, Mrs Thewley! This situation is challenging my reserve, and I'd rather not be challenged any further!'

'Very well!' Mrs Thewley bellowed back, adjusting her goggles and tightening her grip on Duke, who sat placidly on her lap. 'But if we begin to be overtaken by ramblers out on an afternoon hike, you'll forgive me if a let out a hoot or two!'

Daphne hunched forward further in the saddle of the motorcycle. One must always be alert to hazards when behind the wheel, or handlebars, of any moving vehicle. Here in the countryside, for example, one might accidentally clip a partridge, or mow down a badger full pelt. No, no, slow and steady would always win the race. It was her ethos on the road as it was her ethos in her profession.

Although the drizzle had not returned, the December afternoon was a dreary one. Puddles had formed on the narrow country lane, and Daphne slowed almost to halt when she met each one – lest she splash herself, or Mrs Thewley, or, worse still, Duke. Barren hedgerows lined the lane on each side, and every now and then a sparrow flitted from left to right or vice versa.

It was, as Charles had promised, an entirely straight road. Resolutely maintaining second gear, Daphne began to feel more confident in her control of the vehicle. She allowed her mind to wander – in the direction of the young man that the Reverend Mr Smith had told her of. The entire episode had a queer air to it. Who was the young man? What had Mrs Moore noticed about him? Had she caught him red-handed? Or, as Mr Smith had put it, was it merely her instincts that led her to inform Charles that the young man was a nefarious presence? And what of him now? Something was becoming unstuck in her mind. This young man was important, she felt sure of it. Or at the very least, his impact on Charles and the Maybridge Castle household was important.

'I said, Miss King, you appear to have missed our turning!' Mrs Thewley was loudly calling to her.

Abruptly, Daphne came to her senses. No panicked halting or about-turn from her, though. No, no, her precious cargo was not going to be jostled by any sudden or erratic movements. Gently, she squeezed the brakes and pulled the motorcycle to a stop. Then, with utmost care, she manoeuvred the motorcycle so that she was now facing in the direction from which she had just come. Steadily, she turned into small lane that led to their destination: Sheep in a Bucket antiques emporium.

'Very well done, Miss King,' Mrs Thewley complimented her. 'But you might like to know that Duke has been so stupefied and lulled by your pace, that he is now snoring. Yes, I exaggerate not a jot: you have driven a motorcycle with such caution that a cat perching in the sidecar has seen fit to fall asleep.'

Daphne shrugged and retorted that, in fact, cats spent up to three-quarters of their day in slumber, so it was merely a coincidence that Duke was indulging in a nap whilst in the sidecar.

As she dismounted and removed her helmet, Daphne thought it about time to seek the truth from Mrs Thewley.

'Why have you really dragged me here, Mrs Thewley?' she asked, drawing a hand through her hair to disentangle it. 'While I was out, did you spot some kind of clue – some trail that's led us here? Don't tell me: Winifred Roberts had purchased some trinket or other from here the day before her death? Something that might uncover a hidden connection, an obscured motive?'

Mrs Thewley chuckled as she watched Duke hop out of the sidecar and then allowed Daphne to help her out. 'Oh, dearest young duckie,' she replied. 'You give me far more credit than I deserve: I truly do have a passion for collecting porcelain cats, and never miss an opportunity to hunt down new artefacts.'

Daphne's smile faltered. Surely Mrs Thewley was playing out a joke, a prank. She had hauled her here to look for ornaments?

'Oh and I thought it might be a perfect place to tell you about this morning's séance – and what a scene Miss

Helena Rackham made,' Mrs Thewley added. 'Of course we have our eleven o'clock assignation tonight, but you and I both know that so much more might come to light before then.'

24

'Sorry ... Ratty?' Daphne repeated as she leant against the body of the motorcycle. 'That was it? The straw that broke the camel's back, the provocation that sent Helena hurtling from the séance?'

Mrs Thewley nodded and swept a twig from the ground up into her hand. Duke immediately leapt towards it, attacking it with a poise and passion that led Daphne to suppose that he held a personal vendetta against the tree debris.

'Ratty. Who's Ratty? A ... pet? An unloved rodent neglected by a child now seeking to right their wrongs from the afterlife? A ... nickname?' Daphne paused. 'It's a nickname – a not terribly endearing one, but it must be a nickname.'

Mrs Thewley tugged hard at the twig, wrenching it from Duke's claws.

'If it's a nickname, duckie, it's certainly not a nick-name that one would give to one's friend. Not even in affection could one find the moniker "Ratty" acceptable.'

'No,' Daphne ruminated. 'It's a nickname for someone that's . . . looked down on. Not a friend. Someone that's having fun poked at them. The butt of others' jokes.'

Her mind pictured Helena Rackham, her unkempt hair, her toothy grin and all too nervous demeanour.

'Helena Rackham's nickname. *She's* Ratty. Surely. Why else would it send her into such a flap?' Daphne placed her fist into her open palm, pacing around the motorcycle. 'That leaves a couple of questions, of course. Who *called* her Ratty? And how on earth did Madame Marla *know* that someone called her Ratty?'

Mrs Thewley hmmmed. 'Several leaps, there, I suspect, Miss King. It's a theory, I'll grant you that. It's certainly a theory – and not an unlikely one. Ratty evidently carries some . . . sentimental weight for Helena Rackham. Whether she is or is not Ratty – well, that remains to be seen.'

As she finished her sentence, she discarded the twig and led both Duke and Daphne towards the shop entrance. Daphne was about to formulate a counterargument, but was silenced by the sheer volume of . . . *things* that lay inside the shop. And lay was the correct verb. Mountains of trinkets littered the shop: empty glass jars lying on top of wooden signs, lying on top of a tray of marbles, lying on top of a set of binoculars, lying on top of a lamp. All balanced with a precision that boggled Daphne's mind.

'Good afternoon, good afternoon,' a voice from somewhere in the shop boomed. 'Welcome to Asperdale's one and only antiques emporium, Sheep in a Bucket. Margery Dawson at your service. How may I be of assistance to you both this drab and dull afternoon?'

A small woman scurried out from behind a stack of milk pails. She seemed determined to give the impression of eccentricity: upon her head was a knitted bonnet of blue and white stripes, while she was dressed in an open-necked man's shirt with a waistcoat on. Her bottom half was swathed in what appeared to be a Victorian gentlewoman's skirt, complete with bustle and a hem that dragged perilously across the floor. On one hand she had a laced black glove, while on the other perched a bird. On closer inspection, the bird was just one example of the array of taxidermised specimens that were dotted here and there throughout the shop.

'Good day,' Mrs Thewley greeted her. 'Now. I'm in search of something very specific.'

As she explained the details of her desired item, Daphne wandered further into the shop. It was astonishing. A dismantled chandelier was in one corner, around it draped a fur coat. To the left, she could just make out what appeared to be the skeleton of a penny-farthing, no wheels or saddle to confirm this.

She could hear Margery Dawson explaining to Mrs Thewley that she had only relatively recently come into ownership of the shop.

'Matter of fact, I've only been here six weeks. I bought it from an acquaintance of an acquaintance, and, unfortunately for me, the old sod didn't give me a stock inventory. I'm muddling my way through, truth be told, got a lad helping me out here and there.' The woman was stroking the bird in her hand. 'I can't say as I've *seen* any porcelain cats – but that's not to say that they're not *here*. Somewhere.'

Mrs Thewley hid her disappointment by brushing the dust off an oil painting that was lodged between a chipped but still very ornate bed-pan and a horse stir-rup. The painting depicted a battle at sea, something that Daphne suspected was a famous scene, but one that left her yawning.

'This is rather nice – some fine detail there,' Mrs Thewley said as she admired the painting. 'Oh, now, if you've a mind to find out the value of any of this art, you must speak with Mr Moore up at Maybridge Castle. He and his wife, in their previous employment, ran the house of an art dealer over in Liverpool.'

Mrs Thewley must have noticed Daphne's quizzical expression, for she then explained that Mr Moore had told her this on their way back from the trip to Madame Marla and Madame Thelma's house of spectral delights.

'My, my, Mrs Thewley,' Daphne commented. 'You could charm the stars out of the sky, should you set your mind to it. Mr Moore and you appear to be bosom chums now.'

'Pays dividends, Miss King,' Mrs Thewley replied. 'Really, it does.'

Margery Dawson had apparently grown bored of her two customers, and was instead licking her forefinger before then attempting to remove a morsel of dirt from the nautical painting.

After a brief conference, Mrs Thewley and Daphne agreed that they ought to make their way back to Maybridge Castle. It was now half past three, and the light would be fading soon. Goodness knew how Daphne would fare attempting to navigate the motorcycle in the dark.

'We'll be on our way, Mrs Dawson,' Daphne announced, approaching the woman.

Just then, she heard a scuttling to her left. A heavy tramp of feet. There was a closed door, leading off from the section of the shop that appeared to be dedicated to old penny dreadfuls. Looking beneath the doorframe, she could see the movement of shadows. And then she heard a sneeze.

'Is there – is there someone through there?' she asked Margery Dawson.

'Oh, that'll be the lad that's helping me out, William Something or Other. Nice fella, bit quiet, doesn't talk much, but that suits me. P'raps he'll track down some porcelain moggies for you, Mrs T.,' came the reply.

Mrs T.? This was becoming a touch ridiculous. Mrs Thewley, woman of the people, close confidante to Tom, Dick and let us not forget Harry.

It was as Daphne and Mrs Thewley were leaving the shop, and found Duke curled in a ball inside the sidecar, that it struck Daphne. That sneeze. She'd heard it before. She knew that some might argue that a sneeze is a sneeze is a sneeze. But Daphne King begged to differ. For she knew that a sneeze was as personal and unique as a fingerprint, as a drop of blood. And she knew that she'd heard that sneeze before: when Dr John Beaumont was with the police officer after Winifred Roberts's death.

25

The hum of the motorcycle engine (Daphne did not pretend that she had the engine roaring) meant that Daphne could not share her new discovery with Mrs Thewley. It would have to wait until eleven. And besides, Daphne wasn't yet sure what it meant. Could the police constable be helping out Margery Dawson at the Sheep in a Bucket? It seemed improbable. But not impossible; this was, she reminded herself, the countryside.

Dusk was falling as they arrived back at Maybridge Castle. A few ducks had made their way from, presumably, a neighbouring pond, and were strolling along the gravel driveway to the castle. She pulled the motorcycle into the stable and offered her hand to Mrs Thewley.

'Terribly gallant of you, Miss King,' she commented. 'You ought to consider purchasing one of these for yourself, you know. I can see you, weaving your way around buses and black cabs down in London. Weaving exceedingly slowly, of course, but weaving nonetheless.'

It wasn't a bad idea, Daphne thought. Veronica would hate being relegated to the sidecar, but Daphne rather enjoyed the notion. Helmets returned to the broken cupboard, Duke reprimanded for beginning to prowl towards one of the impervious ducks, Daphne and Mrs Thewley went and clanged on the castle door.

It was Mr Moore who answered. He immediately broke into a smile upon seeing Mrs Thewley, and greeted her effusively. To Daphne, he simply offered a small, wordless bow.

There was a hubbub coming from the drawing room. The clock in the hallway told Daphne that it was four o'clock: for Charles, that meant the gin was to be unstoppered, post-haste.

When they entered the room, everyone rose and a chorus of enquiries into the success or failure of Mrs Thewley's mission were heard.

'Alas, I return with only my flesh-and-blood feline,' Mrs Thewley reported. 'The empty spot on my mantelpiece shall remain untouched and desolate for the time being.'

Condolences expressed, Charles poured Mrs Thewley a gin and offered her the prized seat on the sofa beside the fireplace. It really was a rather jolly scene. The Christmas tree was already looking a touch tired – Daphne wondered whether Mrs Moore was watering it sufficiently, as its drooping branches and dropped needles suggested otherwise. Raymond Hammond and John Beaumont were having a tête-à-tête in the corner, John nodding intently at what Raymond was saying. His face had taken on a ruddy hue after the expedition this morning, and his weather-beaten red cheeks were in contrast with his pale white head. His son, Kenneth, was deep in conversation with Helena Rackham, while Eleanor Beaumont was contenting herself with rubbing Duke's belly.

Daphne considered her options. She could ensconce herself among the others, engage in some light interrogations. Fix the beam of her scrutiny on one or two of the guests. Or . . .

'Folks, I'm going to go and freshen up,' she announced, rubbing her eyes and then shaking her hands. 'Feeling a little pooped after that motorcycle adventure – please do excuse me for a little while.'

'At least bring a sherry up with you, Daphne,' Charles suggested. 'Can't have you falling too far behind us all, eh? Especially this devil, Mrs Thewley,' to which the old woman raised her already empty gin tumbler.

Sherry in hand, Daphne turned and left. She looked down and saw that Duke had opted to keep her company. 'Fancy yourself an accomplice snoop, Duke? Well, let's see what you're made of.'

26

When Daphne recounted all of this to Veronica the following week, she wished that she could explain that her reasons for choosing the bedroom she chose were calculated and exacting. That she had weighed up the various factors and the information and hunches she had about each guest, and on the balance of reason had reached a logical conclusion.

As it was, however, she would have to tell Veronica that her decision was based on a simple round of eeny-meeny-miney-mo with Duke.

Her finger landed on the door to the Beaumonts' room. Not a bad outcome. In fact, she reflected, it probably would have been her top choice. There was something about Dr John Beaumont that got her dander up.

In she stepped, and was hit immediately by a wave of perfume. Nauseous though it made her, she waded through the mist. Eleanor Beaumont had installed herself with impressive elan. The desk in the room had been transformed into a cosmetics station, powders and puffs and brushes and implements of unknown purpose lined up uniformly upon the surface. Her bedside table was equally organised and themed. A hairnet, a silk eye mask and a diary sat in a row, in front of which was a small framed photograph of the pair on their wedding day. Eleanor's smile was wide, happiness writ large upon her face. John looked content, solid. A man happy with his lot.

Daphne leafed through the diary, but scanning but a handful of pages left her pessimistic about its use. Eleanor's days seemed filled with chores for the most part, but also shopping trips and chats in Lyons tea rooms with her friends. John, of course, featured heavily. The couple had only started living together as man and wife that summer, and Eleanor seemed fascinated by his daily routine. He appeared to leave very early every day to get to his practice, returning around seven for supper with his new wife. In the run-up to the wedding, the entries were, of course, concerned with dresses and hair appointments. Sprinkled throughout the pages were references to patients and cases that John had alluded to; the boy with the gangrene leg, the Macauley girl.

Daphne replaced the diary. Perhaps she would revisit it, but for now, its usefulness appeared limited.

To John's side of the room. A very different state of affairs. Spartan and bare, the only signs of habitation were a book on his bedside table (a rather dry-looking tome), and a pair of trousers slung over the back of the chair. His suitcase lay closed underneath his side of the bed. Closed, but not locked. Daphne dragged it out and flung the lid back. A few pairs of socks, a scrunched-up shirt. And a notebook. It was well-worn, its brown leather cover peppered with scratches and its pages dog-eared. Daphne picked it up. Inside, John's full name and his practice address. His handwriting was barely legible, but Daphne could make out names – of patients, of conditions. There were crossings-out, ink splotches here and there. For a man who kept his moustache so well clipped, it was a notebook that betrayed a more haphazard side to John Beaumont.

Daphne was flicking through some of the pages, attempting to decipher the writing, when something fluttered out from the notebook. Duke immediately set about pawing at it, and started to gnaw at its edges. A prompt tap on the nose dissuaded him from continuing, and Daphne retrieved it from the floor and perched on the edge of the bed to read it. Typed out on embossed paper, it read:

Dear Dr Beaumont,
This letter is formal notification of your suspension,
pending further investigation. Subsequent to our
conversation last Thursday, 19 November, we are

unable to judge you fit to practise. As you are
aware, complaints have been lodged about your
conduct and the decisions made during your
treatment of Alice Macauley. Please expect to hear
from us again in the next six to eight weeks.
   Yours sincerely,
   Dr Rupert North
   General Medical Council

Daphne re-read the letter twice. John had been suspended – was, she presumed, *still* suspended. Alice Macauley – must be the Macauley girl that Eleanor had ham-fistedly alluded to yesterday. The name had prompted John to momentarily lose his cool, to berate his hapless wife. Eleanor was evidently unaware of her husband's suspension – why else would she make continual references about his job, his passion for medicine? No, she was in the dark, all right. Of that, Daphne was certain. What did this mean for her investigation? John was a man with a secret, but what did it have to do with Winifred's death? Unless . . . Did Winifred somehow know about the black mark by John's name? She certainly seemed eager to prise information out of people when they had met, though perhaps that had been the sherry talking. It was a leap, Daphne thought. A leap to be posited and dissected at her eleven o'clock assignation with Mrs Thewley.

Something stopped Daphne from leaving the Beaumonts' room just yet. Her sense told her that there was more to be uncovered. Another stone to be turned, further worms to observe in their wriggling.

She lay down and looked under the bed.

Aha.

Never overlook the places of least originality.

She stretched her arm and scooped out another envelope, this one far thicker than the last.

There was no name on the front, and it was crumpled and ripped in one corner. The seal had already been broken, and looking inside it, Daphne found that most coveted discovery for investigative reporters: a sizable wad of bank notes. A few hundred was there, Daphne calculated.

Well, well, well.

Amidst the bank notes was also a small fragment of paper. It looked to have been torn from a notebook. Upon it was scrawled a message of malice and intrigue:

I don't want your money, you stupid fool. Keep it. You'll need it to pay for the lawyers when the court case comes.

Mrs Thewley would be pleased with Daphne's findings so far. And she still had time to rifle through one more room.

27

The Hammond men had barely made a dent in the room in which they were staying. Two twin beds were at either end of the room, rather haphazardly placed. The furniture was minimal: no bedside tables, a raggedy carpet in the middle of the room, and a small writing desk by the window. One wardrobe with a lopsided door sat unhappily in the corner.

This room was, evidently, very low on Charles's list of priorities.

She went and glanced out of the window. She was unaccustomed to the absolute darkness here. The sky was a deep black that she had never seen in London, the stars dashes of white that had to compete with the city lights in the metropolis. The Hammonds' window looked out upon the woodland. A creature swooped through the trees. An owl? Daphne would barely know an owl if it bit her on the nose – they were the stuff of legend for such a city-dweller. Gammy-legged pigeons, that was about the extent of the ornithological experiences.

She closed the curtain, though it was evidently a makeshift one that hung crookedly over the window.

This would be an easy search, judging from the austere contents of the ascetic room.

One duffel bag and one suitcase were on each side of the room. She supposed that Raymond's was the suitcase, while she imagined that Kenneth favoured the more youthful accessory of the duffel bag.

The suitcase was a fruitless endeavour, and she rather regretted opting for this vessel first: Raymond's case was full to the brim with off-white y-fronts and matching vests. The underclothes of a middle-aged man would lead her nowhere.

She emptied Kenneth's duffel bag on to the floor. A battered copy of Kant, an old apple core. A jumper with a hole in the sleeve.

And a diary. Hefty and well-thumbed, its black leather cover was stained with grease.

Daphne's hesitation lasted only a few seconds. She had no time for moral quandaries in her line of business. Take your evidence where you could find it, a lesson Daphne had learnt over the course of her dealings.

She began to flick through it from the beginning. Doodles here and there, a few pretentious musings on the nature of existence. Some passages pouring scorn upon rugger matches and varsity drinks. Daphne skipped to the most recent entries. Back from university for the holidays, tedium of Norwich home with Pa overwhelming, et cetera, et cetera. Then she caught a glimpse of Charles's name.

> *How can Pa bear to see that man Charles? A foolish old windbag clowning around with more money than sense. If Charles bloody Howton hadn't been in our lives, then Ma still would be. Him and his avarice. His pig-headed idiocy. If Pa thinks I'll be as spineless as him, forgive and forget, he's even more naive than I thought.*

28

Daphne and Duke made their way back downstairs. The dining room had been decorated with a new centrepiece. It was a festive mixture of holly sprigs and some of the clove-studded oranges that had previously sat upon a mantelpiece.

Daphne positioned herself next to John Beaumont, who frowned slightly when he saw her march towards the chair.

Kenneth Hammond was on her other side, and Mrs Thewley ensured that she was directly opposite Daphne. If glances needed to be exchanged, then all the better.

As Charles entered, he stumbled and leant against the doorframe. Helena Rackham was behind him, and supported him as best she could. Seeing the expressions of alarm on his guests' faces, he waved his hands and said, 'Forgot those damned pills of mine again – where's Moore?'

John Beaumont had risen from his chair, and

volunteered to go and fetch them. Nodding in gratitude, Charles heavily made his way to his chair and plopped into it.

'Charles, I do hope you're not overdoing things,' Daphne said, the concern in her voice evident. Charles's health appeared to be in a state of atrophy.

'No, no, all is well, dear Daphne,' he replied calmly. 'One simply feels things all the more, the older one gets.'

A nod of assent from Mrs Thewley.

Raymond Hammond nodded too, adding, 'From corns to carbuncles, joy to sorrow – it all carries far more import for those among us over the age of sixty!'

His son sipped his wine wincingly. 'You didn't seem to be experiencing too much emotion when that foul woman was making her cruel jokes at your expense last night. Very stoical, Father.'

Daphne looked at the young man. The note of disdain in his voice was unmistakeable. Why this display of displeasure towards his Father? Raymond Hammond took a sip of his own wine, murmured something to his son that sounded very much like, 'Now, now.'

John Beaumont came back, carrying Charles's bottle of pills. Having delivered them, he begrudgingly took his seat next to Daphne once again. Mrs Moore swept in behind him, and began to distribute small plates laden with their starters: a cream and salmon aspic.

Daphne realised that she was ravenous. Miraculously, she had thrown no hunger-induced tantrums this afternoon – one to report back to Veronica in due course. Reaching for her fork, she noticed that Mrs Moore had laid out a two-tined pastry fork at her place. She'd have to use her hands, at this rate.

'Helena, we've not yet had the pleasure of hearing your verdict on the witch burial site,' Daphne said, scooping some of the aspic on to her unwieldy fork. 'Did it live up to expectations?'

Dabbing her mouth with her napkin, Helena considered the question. 'Gosh, yes. Completely so. Its discovery presents an entirely new narrative from the witch trials, one hitherto hidden from view. The women whose remains were found there – we, as yet, have no knowledge of who they were. We know about certain figures persecuted by the witchfinders, by the mobs – but, generally speaking, they pertain mostly to the Pendle witch trials.'

The room was entranced by Helena's passion, her burst of communicativeness.

'Various documents – letters, diaries and such – had indicated that there were trials around the Lakes, but it was only the discovery of a letter last year that pointed more precisely to Asperdale. My entire professional life has been committed to uncovering these women's stories, and now – now I find there are six more voiceless women, goodness knows how many more beyond them.' Helena tapped her front tooth. 'These women – mercilessly hunted, accused, treated inhumanely. Stripped of their dignity and confined to the margins of history. Of course, it was men leading the charge. But cruelty is not confined to men. No, no. Women, as we know, can be just as cruel. Perhaps more so. Targeting the weaker among them for sport.' Helena's eyes were narrowed, she was tapping her wine glass now. She let out a mirth-less chuckle. 'The 1600s, the 1900s – not much has changed, when one really stops and thinks about it.'

The guests silently contemplated Helena's assertion. Various nods rippled around the table.

'In any case! I look forward to reading your findings, Helena,' Daphne said. 'Which reminds me – after dinner I should still very much like to dip my toes into your most recent work.'

The conversation moved on, Kenneth Hammond explaining his dissertation subject to everyone (Daphne couldn't quite follow; though she knew it had something to do with transcending the rational world, which, person-ally, she found perilously close to bunkum), Mrs Moore dutifully ensuring that an empty glass was never seen.

As the evening drew to a close, the clock striking ten, Daphne felt displeased with her performance at dinner.

She was listless, ill-focused. Slapdash. Thoughts of John Beaumont's suspension kept pushing their way into the forefront of her mind. Winifred's twisted limbs were making reappearances in her mind's eye. She was beginning to doubt herself. What if it really *had* been just an accident? Was she allowing herself to conjure up fantastical theories of murder and malice purely for her own amusement? Mrs Thewley agreed that there was something amiss, so it couldn't be just her wild imagination. Could it?

'I say, Charles,' she blurted out, almost against her own volition, 'what'll happen to Winifred's belongings? I take it one of her relatives will be collecting her things? Or providing you with an address to send them on to?'

Charles frowned, either through confusion or irritation that Daphne had chosen to coax the elephant back into the room. 'That's – well, that's a rather good question, Daphne,' he replied. 'One supposes the police will deal with all of that – that they'll arrange such things.'

It was odd, Daphne thought. They had heard not a peep from the police since yesterday.

'Perhaps someone ought to contact them tomorrow – see if there's anything we can do,' Daphne suggested. Charles nodded, looking around to make sure that Mrs Moore was on her way to replenish his wine.

A thought then struck Daphne: Winifred's belongings. Why hadn't she looked at *these* first? Who knew what untold treasures could be among them. You silly little fool, Daphne thought to herself. A misstep that even an investigator in the very infancy of their career ought not make.

It was decided: she had an hour until she needed to be ready to sit down with Mrs Thewley. Plenty of time to slip into Winifred's room and make a survey of the scene.

Daphne paused, closed her eyes. She was coming unstuck. Calm, Daphne. If the cogs began the turn too quickly, chances were that the wheels would come off. And she couldn't have that. She thought back to her motorcycle ride. Steady does it. Helena Rackham's writing, Winifred Roberts's room.

29

Helena had been delighted to deliver into Daphne's hands her most recent piece of work: an essay published in a scholarly journal earlier that year. Daphne deposited it in her bedroom and, changing into her nightwear, waited for the murmurs and rumblings to subside. When she felt safe in the knowledge the other guests had bedded down for the night, she gently twisted her door-knob and closed the door behind her.

Winifred's room lay at the end of the corridor, and creeping towards it Daphne felt a chill. She knew very little about Winifred Roberts, aside from what she had witnessed yesterday evening and what had been reported to her. It felt a violation, using her hairpin to ease Wini-fred's lock open, tiptoeing into the dead woman's room.

But if it would lead to something that pointed towards an enemy among the guests, someone who might have reason to kill her – well, so be it. Winifred's spirit could come and thank her at another of Madame Marla's séances.

Not wishing to alert anyone to her presence by switching on the overhead light, Daphne fished around in her dressing gown pocket for the matches and candle that she had brought with her. As she struck the match, she heard a soft exhalation of breath.

'Hallo, duckie,' Mrs Thewley whispered.

At school, Daphne had enjoyed her physical education sessions. She had been something of a hockey star in her early teens, but it had been in field and track athletics that she had truly excelled. She could still recall the championships in which she claimed the gold in the high jump with an ease that astounded onlookers. This country-conquering high jump was as nothing, however, compared with the height to which Daphne King leapt when, in a dead woman's bedroom, Mrs Amelia Thewley croaked her salutation.

Dropping the candle on to the floor, where it extinguished immediately, Daphne scrambled on her hands and knees to retrieve it. 'For the love of God, Mrs Thewley – why the devil are you hiding in here?'

Through the darkness, Mrs Thewley's hushed reply came. 'Invoking both the Lord above and the lord below – you really are in a flap, Miss King.'

Daphne agreed that, yes, she was in a flap – namely because Mrs Thewley had been lurking like a ghoul in utter darkness in the dead of night.

'Oh, come, come, dear Miss King, surely you can't think you're the only sleuth around here who's handy with a hairpin? Thought it might be rather amusing to lock the door behind me, really make you jump,' Mrs Thewley explained with a chuckle, brandishing a hairpin while Daphne struggled to relight the candle. 'Surely you must have had at least the teensiest weensiest inkling that I might have had the same notion as you? That Winifred Roberts's belongings might well lead us to something . . . tangible? I don't mind admitting that we're both rather groping about in the shadows so far. The pieces are there, all there: it's putting them in the correct shape and in the correct order that's the problem.'

On this point, they were in agreement. Daphne felt as though she was playing one of those silly games that so often appeared at summer fetes, in which the participant, blindfolded or with their sight compromised in some way, puts their hands into a box and must identify the various objects placed within it. She knew that Winifred Roberts had been murdered, in the same way that she knew that jam was jam and that red wine after gin rarely led to anything but headaches and regret.

With the candle finally illuminated once more, Daphne turned her attention to Mrs Thewley. Despite the previous darkness, she had found herself a chair, and was sitting primly, one hand caressing the pearly buttons on her night-dress.

'Well I can't imagine you've discovered much sitting here in the dark, Mrs Thewley,' Daphne began. She felt irritated by Mrs Thewley's presence. She had wanted to conduct this search alone, to have the time and the space to carefully consider Winifred Roberts's belongings and any messages they might communicate. Yet here was Mrs Amelia Thewley, happy as Larry.

'Oh, I only extinguished my candle when I suspected that you might be traipsing your way here, Miss King,' the old woman explained. 'Has anyone told you that you're rather heavy-footed? I don't doubt that they have: quite the commotion when you set yourself about skulking, Miss King. Something you ought to have a dose more practice in.'

Daphne took a deep breath. It would be foolish to expend unnecessary energy in venting her ire at Mrs Thewley. She must remember that the old woman had proved herself useful: she had the entire population of Maybridge Castle eating out of the palm of her hand, so to speak.

She chose to ignore Mrs Thewley's critique of her gait and accompanying advice.

'Does that mean that you've already had a rummage

around, then? Find anything that might help us?' she asked expectantly.

'As a matter of fact, I think I have found *something* that may . . . bridge a gap,' Mrs Thewley replied tantalisingly, waving a small piece of paper in her hand.

Daphne approached and, squinting in the dim light, saw that it was a train ticket. Holding the candle closer, she could make out that it was for a return journey from London Victoria to Surbiton.

Surbiton.

She rifled through her mind. Where and when had Surbiton been mentioned in the preceding two days? She could see a teasing grin slide across Mrs Thewley's face.

'Don't tell me, don't tell me,' she muttered. 'It's on the tip of my tongue . . .'

Mrs Thewley's grin widened, and her eyes were fixed upon Daphne.

'Dr John Beaumont! That's where his practice is!'

Mrs Thewley pointed at her. 'Bingo, dear Daphne: bingo.'

Another piece was clicking into place. Daphne, giddy with the new discovery that Winifred Roberts had been to Surbiton as recently as last Wednesday, according to the ticket, rushed to tell Mrs Thewley all about her earlier snooping escapades and the letter of suspension she had found in the Beaumonts' room.

Surbiton was not, she gathered, a terribly big place. And a woman like Winifred Roberts seemed the type to have her finger very much on the beating pulse of gossip and scandals. Could it be that she and Dr John Beaumont had known each other before their respective visits to Maybridge Castle?

30

Mrs Thewley and Daphne had said their hushed good nights and, using her hairpin, Daphne had locked the door behind her. Mrs Thewley, who prided herself on her own proven finesse with the same tool, had admired Daphne's skills in this regard. Her whispered compliments had gone some way to counterbalancing the thoughts she had aired about Daphne's heavy tread.

Tiptoeing as lightly as she could, Daphne made her way back to her own room. It was now eleven. Fatigue had not reached out its creeping fingers to her; rather, she felt infused with energy and motivation.

She paced around the room, wringing her hands together. She must arrange her thoughts. Compose herself so as to retain the acuity that she felt bubbling within.

What had she uncovered so far? Questions, lots of questions. But also, fragments. Fractured snatches of information and instinct that were, so far, refusing to settle into a clear picture.

There was Cousin Charles's missing cane. It could easily have been the weapon used to kill Winifred Roberts. Did that mean that Cousin Charles had wielded it in anger? Not necessarily. And, as she had been observing, Cousin Charles was not in particularly rude health. Did he have the strength to swing a cane with such great force? It seemed doubtful. But not impossible.

Then there was Dr John Beaumont. A doctor hiding his professional difficulties from his wife. A man whose manner bespoke unresolved tensions and festering wounds. And now she had a train ticket which indicated that Winifred Roberts had been to the very town in which John Beaumont's medical practice was.

Daphne paused. When she framed it so baldly, what did she, in fact, actually possess by way of proof or clues? A rather flimsy offering, she thought.

She kept circling that sneeze. Why was that presenting itself so prominently among her thoughts? Goodness knew. Perhaps she was more tired than she had supposed.

Slinging her dressing gown on the back of a chair, Daphne decided that a decent night's sleep would grant her a fresh-eyed perspective on occurrences tomorrow. She clambered into the bed and, putting on her glasses, looked again at the essay that Helena Rackham had penned for the periodical.

She was rather in the mood for some macabre tales of

witchcraft, and, settling down, she found herself impressed by the muscularity and poise of Helena's prose. Nothing flowery or overly lurid, just brutal facts set out in unvarnished words.

She was enjoying reading about the sorry story of one Maria Sutton, by all accounts something of a village outcast who had found herself on the wrong side of the area's witchfinder. He was a stout and malicious man named Wheeler; according to Helena's research, he could have been responsible for the abominable murders of dozens of women in the 1600s who had been accused of witchcraft.

It was when Daphne reached the small biography of Helena Rackham at the end of the article, that Daphne read three words which stopped her dead. Unconsciously, she held her breath. She traced her finger over the sentence, two, three times:

Helena Rackham attended Girton College, Cambridge where she read History. Prior to university, her education began in earnest at Brindlecombe Girls' School, whose motto, *gloria in labore*, encouraged her to forge her academic career.

There it was, in black-and-white. *Gloria in labore*. Infrequently did Daphne's daily life hinge upon Latin school mottos. So when she did encounter such oddities, they remained in her memory. And she had heard this motto just yesterday: Winifred Roberts had thrown it into the conversation, sneering at her school motto. Winifred Roberts and Helena Rackham had attended the same school.

31

A cockerel sounded the alarm for daybreak. Daphne could also make out the discordant snorting of the three pigs in their field. She peeped through the curtain and saw Mr Moore happily sloshing their breakfast into their trough. Country life was something for which she could never quite muster excessive zeal. Of course, she appreciated the fresh air, could admire nature as and when it deserved admiration. Majestic oaks, for example. Elegant herons. The odd small- to medium-sized mammal. Bluebells, yes, there were the bluebells too. All very well in small doses, or in conjunction with dashing across London to get from one soirée to the next. Yes, she was perfectly happy to visit a green space and look upon its plenitude with gratitude. But she would then quite like to get back to Fleet Street, dodging pedestrians in order to make it back to the office on time for an editorial meeting. The cut and thrust of it, that's what Daphne thrived on.

She sighed. It was already Sunday morning. One more night and then she would be juddering her way back down to London on the train.

One more night. That was all she had.

It was eight o'clock. She had formulated her plan after reading Helena Rackham's essay last night. Now she must set about putting it into action. Hastily, she discarded her pyjamas and flung on her day clothes. Her corduroy slacks had seen better days, but sartorial matters lay at the very bottom of her priorities. On most days, in fact, but on this particular day especially. Buttoning up her blue shirt, she glanced in the mirror and resolved herself: time was running out. She was going to have to confront those above whose names floated a suspicious question mark. Perhaps it was an endeavour for which she ought to enrol Mrs Thewley's assistance. She had heard tell that the police often employed a strategy whereby one officer remained brusque, abrasive, while the other coaxed and wheedled a suspect. It might be a technique worth taking for a spin.

Descending the stairs, she could hear Mrs Thewley's voice ringing out in the dining room already. Now, Daphne, it doesn't do to be jealous. It can't be helped that they all wish to fall at Mrs Thewley's feet in adoration, while so far she herself remained a rather distant, inscrutable figure. No matter.

She opened the dining-room door and quickly realised that she was the last of the guests to appear for
breakfast. The rest of the guests were assembled eagerly
around one side of the table, all peering at something
which was concealed from Daphne by the mass of their
bodies.

'Can you credit it? This has been languishing in the
Moores' living quarters for seven years!' Mrs Thewley
was chuckling, to murmured responses and a 'golly!'
from Helena Rackham.

'Well, well,' Daphne said by way of announcing her
arrival, 'what do we have here, then? Sounds rather
intriguing.'

Kenneth Hammond and his father stood aside so that
Daphne could see what was causing such a commotion.
It was a painting, a dulled bronze frame around it. The
picture was a rather lovely rendering of a hay field, a few
bucolic figures dotted through it, scythes in hand. Swirls
of blues and yellows led one's eye through the scene, a
blissful rural idyll in summer. Daphne could almost feel
the pollen attacking her sinuses.

'How . . . lovely,' she remarked, uncertain as to how
effusive she ought to be with her praise. 'Where did you
say it came from, Mrs Thewley?'

The old woman explained that, after her conversation
with Mr Moore yesterday in which she had shared her

passion for painting and he had mentioned that his previous employer was the art dealer in Liverpool, Mr Moore had happened upon this in his rooms.

'A gift from this previous employer chappie when the Moores decided to move on from his household and come to Cumbria,' Mrs Thewley added. 'Fancy that – a light positively smothered beneath a bushel!'

'Funny, the things people store away and never think about,' Eleanor Beaumont said. 'Things just hidden . . . in plain sight, almost!'

Daphne refrained from giving an ironic snort. She sat down next to Mrs Thewley and reached for a slice of toast. Mrs Moore filled her tea cup and Daphne nodded her thanks. 'What a fetching painting that is, Mrs Moore.'

Mrs Moore curtseyed. 'Why, yes, Miss King. It's a pretty one. Mr Archibald – that is to say, our employer before Mr Howton – he had all sorts knocking about in his house.'

Evidently, art was the prompt needed to wring some conversation from Mrs Moore.

She went on, 'There was this one – oh, it was by the Dutch fellow . . . the one with the ear. Well, without the ear.'

Mrs Thewley furnished her with the name, and Mrs Moore continued.

'So yes, it was by this Van Gogh. Mr Archibald, he

says it's one that's never, ever been in a museum or a gallery. Only seen by people visiting Mr Archibald. Very proud of it, he was. Shame he's fallen upon such hard times now – word reached us that he's going about selling all of his art. His pride and joy, that collection was.'

Mrs Moore appeared to remember that she was, in fact, supposed to be adhering to that age-old maxim: domestic staff should be seen and not heard. Daphne never did like it, but she could see a blush spreading across Mrs Moore's face.

'Here's you all wishing to eat your breakfast in peace, here's me blathering on. I do apologise.' With that, she proffered one of her now infamously cumbersome curtseys, and scuttled out of the room.

'Well I'll be a jack-rabbit's auntie,' Mrs Thewley uttered. 'A secret Van Gogh, just hanging in the dining room of a Liverpudlian art dealer? That's something you don't hear every day. I've half a mind to find out what the asking price is.'

Daphne watched Mrs Thewley and couldn't quite determine the authenticity of her reaction. Would Mrs Thewley really be in the position to purchase a lost Van Gogh painting? Daphne had the distinct impression that the old woman, while of means, certainly, was a modest widow living the life of a modest widow. Not the life of an art fiend pursuing a lost Dutch masterpiece. Once again, Daphne found herself repeating the notion that one really did never know.

Kenneth Hammond was leafing through a magazine as he continued with his breakfast. 'Hang about,' he blurted. 'Isn't this you, Mrs Thewley?'

He held up the magazine, and there, indeed, was a double-page spread with the headline, 'Debunker seeks to ruin Spiritualism's reputation.' Beneath it was a photograph of Mrs Thewley and Duke, two sets of eyes gleaming out of the page mischievously.

Mrs Thewley confirmed that this was the interview that she had conducted with *Spiritualism Now* two months ago. Daphne asked Kenneth to pass it to her, and as she scanned the page, she noticed pencil marks underlining several sentences in the article.

'I say, Kenneth – where did you get this?' she asked.

'Oh it was just . . . lying around somewhere, I'm not certain. Possibly the kitchen? I came down for a glass of milk in the night, that's right. And it was on one of the shelves.'

She looked again at the underlined sections. She would hold on to this.

Chewing a bite of her toast, Daphne glanced around at the guests. 'Now, I've a proposal for you all. This famed Maybridge Castle maze – who's game for exploring it? Charles insists on everyone keeping their distance from that rusty aviary, but I don't see any reason why we can't go the long way round and have morning promenade in the maze. See if we can't track down any of the apparitions that apparently stalk it, morning, noon and night.' She took another bite of her toast. Where was Charles, she wondered. Probably out engaging the services of more clairvoyants.

There were some scattered nods around the table. To her surprise, by far the most enthusiastic assent came from Dr John Beaumont.

He smoothed his moustache, took a measured sip of his tea. 'Well I think that sounds like a fine idea, Daphne. Very fine indeed. The only hitch is that, before you came down, a few others suggested a trip to that beach just over the hill. Eleanor's terribly keen – aren't you darling?'

Eleanor nodded and let out a squeal. 'Now, I know it'll be freezing, absolutely perishing down there, but I do so want to get my toes in the Irish Sea! Imagine what Barbara and the girls will say!'

Daphne smiled wanly. Then a thought struck her. What would Barbara and the girls say if they knew about John Beaumont's suspension? As far as Daphne could tell, the approval of Barbara and the girls was something that Eleanor kept uppermost in her mind. What if she *did* know about her husband's straits? And knew that

Winifred Roberts knew? Would that be enough to persuade a woman like Eleanor to . . . bump someone off? Daphne dismissed the idea. Nonsense. Outlandish guff. Surely?

Raymond Hammond, pipe in mouth, was searching his pockets for a lighter. 'Kenneth and I were also rather eager to see the beach; I'm told the view across the sea is superb.'

Helena Rackham informed the group that she would be going back to the woodland burial grounds – her initial observations yesterday required further probing.

'So it's settled then,' Daphne declared. 'John, Mrs Thewley and I will navigate the maze.'

'Not forgetting Duke as well, Miss King,' Mrs Thewley added, plopping a lump of sugar into her tea. 'He possesses the most miraculous sense of direction – he'll have us to the centre in three shakes of a monkey's tail. Possibly even two.'

Aware of time's mocking hand incessantly ticking onwards, Daphne inelegantly gobbled down two more slices of toast. If she was going to miss lunch again today – and by Jove she hoped she would be able to avoid that lamentable situation – then she ought to be prepared.

Daphne, Mrs Thewley and John Beaumont folded their napkins upon their breakfast plates, wished a pleasant beach morning to the others – and a fruitful stint of burial site labouring to Helena – before heading to the hallway to bundle on their coats. There was a slight frost upon the ground today, Daphne had noticed when peering out of her bedroom window. December chills making themselves known.

'Charles tells me there's a splendid statue in the middle of the maze,' Daphne remarked as the trio buttoned buttons and affixed scarves, their coats handed to them by Mr Moore. 'A noble canine, so he tells me. Keeping watch over Maybridge Castle and all who set foot within her. By the sounds of it, rather similar to a very striking statue Veronica and I saw in Central Park when we were in New York earlier this year. Oh, what's his name, he's an adorable sled dog . . .'

'Balto, I believe, Miss King,' Mr Moore chipped in. 'Endurance, fidelity, intelligence, that's him. Heroic-looking beast, isn't he?'

Daphne fumbled slightly with her buttons and glanced up at Mr Moore. He must have caught something in her gaze, for he instantly spoke again.

'So I understand. From . . . reading about such things. In a book.'

'Let me guess: a book, perchance, on the shelves in your previous employer's house, the art collector's den in Liverpool?' Daphne asked.

Mr Moore held her stare. His face back to its impassive blankness.

'I believe it was, in fact, a library book that I borrowed,' he replied, an unmistakeable terseness to his voice.

'Oh here you are, you silly cat,' Mrs Thewley exclaimed. Daphne turned to see Duke padding leisurely down the stairs. 'He's been galloping around all over the place this morning, hiding from me – you diabolical little imp, you.'

'Will Duke be joining us then, Mrs Thewley?' John asked, smiling. 'I don't fancy our chances without a feline navigator on hand – or on paw, I should say – to offer guidance.'

It was agreed that, yes, Duke would be joining them – but that all three must keep a close eye on the naughty young lad. Mrs Thewley had known him to dart off in pursuit of a bluebottle, never mind anything so exotic as the red squirrels that were to be found in Asperdale.

Mr Moore nodded a farewell to the small party as they stepped outside.

'And do tell Cousin Charles, when he emerges, the old lazy bones, that we'll be back for lunch.'

32

At the first suggestion of wildlife, Duke had sprinted away from his companions at great speed. Daphne watched as he slowed to a prowl, though what he had in his sights she couldn't tell.

Giving the aviary as wide a berth as possible, Daphne, Mrs Thewley and John Beaumont arrived at the maze. Although unkempt and somewhat unwieldy, the winding paths and tall hedges were still impressive – and somewhat intimidating. The gravel crunched beneath their feet as they approached. Daphne could see what looked like a kite swooping in the sky above, its wingspan allowing it to glide effortlessly as it scanned the ground beneath for prey.

Daphne's breath appeared as fog before her as she said, 'Right-o: away we go, I suppose.'

She had been wrong-footed when John Beaumont had so eagerly stated that he wanted to join her in the maze. She hadn't been expecting this newfound keenness to spend time with her – particularly when yesterday her every utterance appeared to get his dander up. No wonder, really, she reflected. For that was precisely what she was hoping to do. Now, the question was: when should she reveal her knowledge of his suspension? And, further to that, how would she broach the Winifred Roberts angle? The train ticket existed, yes, but what did it prove? That she had once – possibly only ever once – visited a town where John Beaumont happened to practise medicine? In the cold light of day – and cold was the light – it was insubstantial at best, grasping at worst.

And there was this new hypothesis making itself known in her mind. Something based on fleeting remarks and apparently inconsequential comments—

'So, Dr Beaumont,' Mrs Thewley began. 'A question, if I may. Why were you suspended from practising medicine? And when are you going to inform your wife of this rather unfortunate turn of events?'

Daphne and John stopped abruptly, as if a phantasm had just jumped from behind a hedge, replete with clanking chains and white sheet.

'Oh, I do apologise,' Mrs Thewley had also stopped. 'That was two questions, wasn't it?'

What the devil? Mrs Thewley was supposed to be playing the gently-gently part. It was Daphne who ought to be launching attacks. Yet here Mrs Thewley was, sledgehammer in hand when she was supposed to be wielding but a nutcracker.

'Now, look here, Mrs Thewley,' Daphne began in affront, her irritation transmogrifying into indignation, 'just who do you—? What kind of a—?'

John Beaumont held up his hands.

'It's all right, Daphne – Mrs Thewley,' he said. There was a softness to his voice that Daphne had only detected previously when he was speaking with his wife. 'I've been wondering when you were going to ask me outright – all those looks you've been giving me. That hoo-ha with those bloody Tarot cards yesterday.'

Daphne frowned and looked at Mrs Thewley, who simply shrugged.

'My dear duckie Daphne,' the old woman said. 'We don't have inexhaustible time on our side – the question had to be asked.'

John looked around at the hedges, a deep exhalation of breath hanging in the air before him. 'How did you know? About the suspension?'

Daphne confessed to her investigation of his room, to which he simply sighed. He appeared a man resigned, no further fight within him.

'It was a stupid mistake. I was tired, wasn't paying attention properly – missed something I should have caught. It happens all the time. Only usually it's a minor thing – this time, the girl . . . the girl died. Because I was too lazy or stupid or tired or all three – to spot what was glaringly obvious. So. I was suspended,' he stated, putting his hands in his pockets. 'It's as simple as that. And I haven't told Eleanor because I can't face the shame – she thinks she's married a stable, strong husband, with an income and respect and expertise. I couldn't face her knowing that, in fact, she's married a blundering fool and there's no money coming into the house.'

Daphne watched as he unspooled all the embarrassment and the burden he'd been keeping to himself. He seemed oddly relieved to be telling them, here in the frosty maze at Maybridge Castle.

Mrs Thewley put a hand on his shoulder. 'Painful though it may be, the truth is far preferable to storing this secret. It will fester and rot, and it will be putrid and cause untold damage to your relationship. I've seen the way your bride looks at you. She loves you for far more than your stability and a regular income. Trust in her love for you.'

Mrs Thewley was playing the role of doting old lady dispensing pearls of wisdom and timeless truths. She was embracing that role with exceptional panache.

'What about Winifred Roberts?' Daphne interjected. She'd had quite enough chatter about trusting in love for one day, thank you very much.

John's eyes narrowed. 'That infernal shrew.'

Aha, Daphne thought. Tears and shame for the wife; insults and cold glares for the dead woman.

'I gather that's a rather popular opinion of her,' Daphne said. 'Care to explain why it is that you in particular share this opinion?'

John's eyes travelled to meet Mrs Thewley's; she nodded, as if granting him permission to speak with Daphne.

'She – oh, she's – she *was* a horrible woman. Truly horrible. That first evening here, she clocked me. I didn't know who on earth *she* was, but oh, she knew me, all right.' Bitterness dripped from John's words. 'She'd been in Surbiton – some party or other, I don't know, I don't go to these things. Winifred Roberts, of course, of course, had a pal on the GMC. Rupert North – the very man who issued my suspension. It appears that he takes confidentiality very lightly – very lightly, indeed. Told Winifred about the dramatic case he'd been assigned – no doubt trying to impress the woman.'

Daphne frowned. It was a case of sheer coincidence? Winifred Roberts just so happened to be at a party where she just so happened to be told about John's predicament. Bunkum, surely.

'Go on, dear,' Mrs Thewley said encouragingly. 'These awful coincidences happen more often than one supposes.'

'As soon as she heard my name on that first night here, she had the most hideous smile. Like a . . . like a hyena or something. Vicious, cruel. She found an opportunity to speak to me alone – I was, I can't remember, going to the WC most likely – and the taunts she threw at me. For no reason, other than her own lurid entertainment. Could tell from my face that Eleanor had no idea about it all. Suggested that, if she had any more sherry, she might accidentally let slip to her.'

They were getting somewhere, Daphne thought. The anger was making itself known in his voice, she could see how full of rage he still was. This woman had belittled and scorned him – and threatened to humiliate him in front of his wife.

'So, well, I was livid. I told her she wouldn't get away with it. That if she did anything, there'd be consequences.'

Daphne and Mrs Thewley's eyes met: the whispering in the corridor when they had both first arrived at Maybridge Castle.

'And? What were those consequences, John? What did you decide to do?' Daphne waited with bated breath. Was this it?

A few seconds passed. John turned away from them both. Brought his hands to his face. Through his fingers, he groaned, 'Nothing.'

Taking his hands from his face, he continued, 'I did absolutely nothing. I didn't even have any . . . well any ideas of what I could do to stop her, or to teach her a lesson if she did say anything to Eleanor. I just . . . let the evening happen. Let her have the run of the place. So weak, so spineless. Here was a woman threatening to do her best to destroy my wife's respect for me – and I didn't lift a finger to do anything.'

Daphne eyed him carefully. The deflation looked real. The evident sense of worthlessness. John Beaumont wasn't a murderer. He wasn't capable of it.

'Oh, dear Dr Beaumont,' Mrs Thewley was saying in consoling tones. 'What *could* you have done?'

'Well, you could have bashed her on the head and then pushed her down the stairs, for one,' Daphne drawled, kicking a stone and shoving her hands into her pockets.

'Now, now,' Mrs Thewley said. 'Is Miss King becoming impatient and petulant? Where is the dogged crime reporter who latches on to a story and never lets it go? Hmm? The ardent believer in truth and justice who sees through foibles and vanities in order to cut to the heart of the matter? Is she going to smile? I think she might be going to smile.'

Mrs Thewley's coaxing was too amusing to resist. And the flattery certainly didn't go amiss.

'Very well. Onwards. We shall continue, Mrs Thewley, in our pursuit of revelation,' Daphne acquiesced.

John looked from one woman to the other. 'You two honestly thought that I might have ... *killed* Winifred Roberts?'

Daphne shrugged her shoulders. 'You were one line of enquiry that we were pursuing – but I think we are sufficiently satisfied that you weren't behind this, John. I'm starting to think things are rather more complicated than we first—'

'Darrrrrrling!' came a trilling voice. 'Oh husband miiiiiine!'

Daphne looked up to see Eleanor Beaumont trotting towards the maze. An impressive woolly bobble hat was atop her head, and her hands were contained in what appeared to be a fur muff. Evidently, Eleanor Beaumont had returned rather promptly from the beach.

'No time like the present, Dr Beaumont,' Mrs Thewley said.

A flash of panic streaked across the doctor's face. It was quickly superseded by an expression of placidity. Calm acceptance.

Eleanor's pace slowed as she neared the trio.

'John, you look ever so pale – I knew you didn't eat enough at breakfast, let's get you back. A rasher of bacon, p'raps some sausages, few gulps of sugary tea, see you right as rain.' She was speaking with alarming rapidity.

John nodded at Mrs Thewley then approached his wife. Clasping her by the shoulders, he stilled her.

'Whatever's the matter, John? You're – you're starting to worry me. Mrs Thewley, Miss King, what's going on?' Eleanor asked in agitation.

'Darling Eleanor, I need to tell you – tell you something awful.'

Eleanor's face was drained of colour. 'What – what do you mean? Something awful? Something . . . what?'

Her eyes darted around from her husband to Mrs Thewley to Daphne.

'Would you like to take her inside, duckie?' Mrs Thewley asked gently.

'No, I'm not going anywhere. Not until somebody tells me what – is – going – on!' Eleanor's voice was wavering unsteadily.

'It's, well, it's about work,' John began, his hands still on Eleanor's shoulders. 'That Macauley girl. I . . . I wasn't entirely truthful. The fact is . . . I didn't save her. I didn't help her. I made a bloody stupid mistake. And now she's dead and I'm suspended. I'm to be investigated. I – I don't know what the outcome will be. I'm sorry.'

Daphne was moved by the simplicity of John's words. The evident heartbreak that had overtaken him.

She was also moved by Eleanor's response. Moved to thought and to a niggling sense of alertness. For Eleanor Beaumont barely reacted at all. Her face was a blank. Had she even blinked?

Daphne glanced at Mrs Thewley, who was also steadily observing Eleanor. The woman now cleared her throat and adjusted her incongruously jolly woollen hat.

'Well, darling, that's – that's unfortunate. Nothing we can't manage though,' she said evenly.

John seemed taken aback. 'That's – that's all? That's terribly understanding of you, darling, but . . . don't you want to . . . ask me any questions? Aren't you . . . angry that I've kept it from you?'

Eleanor shook her head. 'No. I – I love you and that's all that matters. We'll just have to tighten our belts, save up money for lawyers and whatnot when it comes to court.'

John embraced his wife warmly and began uttering words of gratitude and affection.

Daphne narrowed her eyes. *Save up money for lawyers when it comes to court.*

The note. The money in the bedroom.

'What a lucky man I am, to have such a wife by my side. Look at you – you're so composed, so calm,' John exclaimed.

'That's because she already knew about your secret, John,' Daphne stated measuredly.

Eleanor froze once more, her face an image of shock. She began babbling incredulously, a garble of half-words and incoherent vowel sounds that Daphne couldn't decipher.

'That was a generous sum you offered Winifred Roberts to keep her quiet. Very loyal of you, Eleanor. Noble, really. Protecting your husband. But she threw your money back in your face, didn't she?' Daphne's tone remained composed.

John looked at his wife in confusion. 'Excuse me, Miss King, look here – I don't know what notion you've cooked up, but—'

'She was a spiteful witch, that woman,' Eleanor said. Her eyes fixed on Daphne. She turned to her husband. 'I knew about it. I knew you'd been getting those letters – and I knew that you weren't telling me the truth about them. I'm no fool, John, though people might take me for one. I just . . . I wanted to know what they were. I took one of those letters, a month ago. Read all about it. Then . . . when we came here . . . that woman. I could tell that she was a bad egg. Then I heard her taunting you. So – so I thought I could shut her up. I had that cash on me because I was going to treat you – take you to Scotland after this for Christmas. Give you a chance to speak to me about everything. She didn't want the money though. She was enjoying the drama of it all.'

John was speechless, his mouth agape.

Mrs Thewley interjected, 'So you wanted to protect your husband – keep him safe, keep him out of her way. But it didn't work, did it, duckie?'

'When she didn't want your money, what did you do, Eleanor?' Daphne asked coolly.

It took a moment for the penny to drop. Eleanor realised what she was being asked.

'No – no, that's not what happened. I didn't *kill* her. I'm not – I'm not a *monster*. I just . . . I just thought I could take John away to Scotland after all. It was stupid to offer that creature the money.' She began crying, softly at first. John took her in his arms. 'I just wanted . . . to . . . show you . . . that I can . . . I can be useful, John.'

Mrs Thewley and Daphne glanced at one another. Was this performance persuading either of them? It appeared that it was.

Before Daphne could say anything more, Mrs Thewley cried out.

'Duke! Oh, here you are again. What have you got there, you naughty thing?'

Duke slunk towards the figures, his head slightly lowered. Daphne thought she could detect a slight limp in his steps. As implied by Mrs Thewley's question, there did seem to be something in Duke's mouth. Something rather sizable. And feathery.

He approached Mrs Thewley and deposited his gift at her feet. It was, as Daphne had suspected, a bird.

'Oh Duke, don't you know you're not supposed to be marauding Maybridge Castle and massacring its wildlife?' Mrs Thewley berated the cat. 'Especially not, if I'm correct, those precious finches that Charles told us about.'

Cousin Charles would be beside himself when he found out about this. And so too would Mr Moore, given as he appeared to be the expert ornithologist.

Mrs Thewley left the dead bird on the ground but scooped Duke into her arms, looking him straight in the eyes as she continued her scolding. She was stroking him on the back of his head when Daphne noticed it.

The blood.

'Mrs – Mrs Thewley,' she began, 'I don't wish to alarm you, but it appears that – well Duke seems to be bleeding.'

Mrs Thewley looked at her hand, the palm of which was now sticky with blood. She suppressed a scream. 'Duke! My Duke, where are you hurt? What's happened?'

Daphne quickly approached and began to assist Mrs Thewley in inspecting the cat. There was too much blood for a bird as small as a finch. If there was a wound capable of producing this much blood, they would need to locate it – quickly.

The two women crouched on the ground – a challenge in itself for Mrs Thewley – and continued to search about Duke's body for the injury. He, meanwhile, appeared to be enjoying the search very much – his purring grew in intensity and he rolled appreciatively as they gently prodded and parted his fur.

Daphne stood up, frowning. There was no cut, not even a scratch. Duke was unscathed, limping a little, yes, but there was no visible injury.

She gripped Mrs Thewley by the shoulder.

'The blood – it's not Duke's. It's someone else's.'

33

Logic dictated that Duke had come from the aviary: the finches were, Mrs Thewley and Daphne both agreed, nesting in there. So to the aviary they headed, marching briskly with a confused John and Eleanor Beaumont trailing behind them.

The rusted edifice now shimmered slightly, frost glittering in the December morning sun.

Daphne found her way to what appeared to be the main entrance to the chambers within.

'Mrs Thewley, I rather think it best if you stay out here,' Daphne murmured to her companion. 'Lord knows what might lie within. Where there's blood, there's usually something gruesome, as far as I've learnt.'

A sound came from Mrs Thewley, something halfway between a snort and a tut.

Daphne, puzzled, turned to face her.

'Miss King, in all of my seventy-five years on this

green earth, just how many scenes of a gruesome bent do you suppose I've encountered? Willingly or otherwise?'

Daphne felt herself blush, heat creeping along her neck – despite the chill in the air.

'And how many of those gruesome scenes do you suppose have left me swooning, bilious, haunted in my nightmares?' A wry smile danced upon Mrs Thewley's lips, and she stroked Duke slowly. 'The answer to that is precisely: one. And that was when my neighbour and best friend, poor Jane Simmons, fell out of a tree and broke her shin bone in 1868. Despite the not inconsiderable nausea that I initially experienced, I still managed to fashion a splint, talk sense into her and make her comfortable before alerting her mother to the accident. Believe me when I tell you, Miss King, that there's not much that can shock me.'

Daphne stuttered her reply. 'Quite – yes, I do apologise, Mrs Thewley, that suggestion was somewhat—'

'Patronising? Infantilising? A terrible underestimation of my mettle?' Mrs Thewley was enjoying prodding Daphne.

Daphne was on shaky ground. One might argue, of course, that two pairs of eyes surveying a scene could only be more useful than one. Experience, however, told Daphne that she needed solitude and silence. No companion asking questions, pointing out details that might distract her. She would need to muster some tact and charm.

'All of the above, Mrs Thewley, for which I can only implore you to forgive me,' she began. 'That said, we have very little idea of what we're dealing with in this precise moment. Anyone could be wandering, lurking, skulking – in the aviary and out here. I understand that you're in no need of any mollycoddling. But what I do need is someone to stand guard here and keep a lookout for anyone or anything that might have caused blood to spill. Can we agree on that?'

Mrs Thewley's eyebrows were raised. 'I'm impressed, Miss King. You've handled a cantankerous and pig-headed old woman with composure and self-assurance. Stand guard I shall. With Duke and the Beaumonts here as my assistants.'

Minor dispute resolved, Daphne pulled back the iron gate and stepped into the aviary. The density of the climber clutching at the iron structure meant that little light entered the aviary. It was colder in here, too. She pulled her coat tighter.

The ground of the aviary was littered with dead leaves from the climbers, and there was little sign of any industry within. Odd, she thought. She understood that Moore had taken it upon himself to restore and revive the aviary. Bird waste was splattered here and there, but there was no chirruping: an unnerving silence pervaded the edifice.

Then she spotted the paw prints – paw prints of blood. Duke's pathway. He must have leapt – or rather scrambled – over the gate to get in.

She followed the prints into the chamber to the right of the main one. It was a little smaller, and even darker.

Daphne gasped.

There, lying on the ground, was Charles's cane.

And beside it, Charles. Bloodied and still.

She ran over and dropped to her knees, calling his name and checking his neck. There was no pulse. Charles was dead.

The left side of his head had been struck, blood pooled around it.

His face was frozen in an expression of horror, his eyes widened in fear.

Daphne took a deep breath and inched towards him. She closed his eyes.

Cousin Charles, killed. Murdered at Maybridge Castle. By the same person who had killed Winifred Roberts; she had been right, it was the cane all along.

Tears blurred her vision. A sickening, twisting knot formed in her stomach. Charles had been such a kind man, so generous and so good-natured.

He had unquestioningly welcomed her into the family, treating her as though she really was his cousin.

Veronica. She would have to tell Veronica. Oh, this would break her heart.

She stood up, took a deep breath. Calm, composed Daphne King. That's who she had to be right now. Circumstances called for it, and she'd be damned if she'd let anything evade her now.

She looked around the chamber where Charles lay. Something peculiar. Although the creeper was just as prolific in this chamber, grasping the roof just as it did in the main chamber – there were only dead leaves on one patch of the ground. In the corner, a space of, she estimated, five foot by five foot lay bare. Not a single leaf upon the ground. Something had been there. A crate? Something that had been moved very recently. She crouched down by the bare patch of ground and noticed something else: tiny flecks of blue were splattered intermittently on the ground. The paint on the edifice had been red, as evidenced by the remaining flakes upon the iron columns – so this blue pigment, whatever it was, couldn't have originated there.

In a practised scan, Daphne looked around for any other noteworthy observations. Nothing else. Just the bare patch, the blue flecks. And Charles's dead body.

She walked slowly out of the aviary, her feet growing heavier with each step.

Mrs Thewley stood with the Beaumonts.

'What – what is it, Daphne?' Mrs Thewley had never called her by her Christian name. Had never eschewed formality.

She looked at her, tears springing again to her eyes. 'It's Cousin Charles . . . he's – he's dead.'

Mrs Thewley rushed to her with all the speed she could, and enveloped her in an embrace. Daphne let the tears flow, but then resolved to take mastery of her emotions. She gently released herself from Mrs Thewley's arms, and wiped her face with her sleeve.

John Beaumont asked what had happened.

'He's been murdered. Struck on the head – just like Winifred Roberts. It's a horrific way to go. The look in his eyes . . .' She trailed off, flinching as she recalled the expression on his dead face. Eleanor Beaumont let out a shriek, and John huddled her close to his body.

Mrs Thewley made to embrace her once more, but Daphne took a step backwards. She must be steelier than ever now. She must take charge. Sort out this mess. She had to let Veronica know that she was going to find the truth. Cousin Charles would have justice.

'John, Eleanor – go to the hallway and call the police. Make sure they get here soon – as fast as they can. I'll have stern words for whoever these ninnies are.' Daphne issued her instructions without faltering. She knew what needed to be done. 'Mrs Thewley, when we get back to the castle, you check the ground floor, I'll do upstairs. We must establish as quickly as possible just who is here and who isn't. Eleanor – have Kenneth and Raymond come back from the beach yet?'

Eleanor shook her head, gulping back a few sobs as she did so. 'I – I – well I don't know. They might be – but, well, I don't know . . .'?'

Daphne balled her right hand into a fist, enveloping it in her left. Her breath was becoming ragged. She must regain control of herself. Of the situation.

She glanced at Mrs Thewley.

'It is vitally important that we determine who's been on the grounds in the last . . . half an hour,' she continued.

Mrs Thewley held Daphne's gaze, a steely glint in the old woman's eyes.

Daphne had learnt to trust her intuition, the flights of fancy or the leaps of faith that her mind took in moments of crisis or desperation. She knew, looking at Mrs Thewley, that her mind had darted to the same place.

The diary in Kenneth Hammond's bedroom.

'If Charles bloody Howton hadn't been in our lives, then Ma still would be . . . If Pa thinks I'll be as spineless as him, forgive and forget, he's even more naive than I thought.'

34

She would wait until after the police had arrived. She would place the long-distance call to the Palace Hotel, New York once she had spoken with the police. Although, she thought . . . it was nine thirty in the morning in Asperdale, which would make it . . . four thirty in the morning in New York. Veronica would either still be revelling in the city, or she would be lost in a deep sleep in her bed. Telling Veronica would have to come later, then.

Mrs Thewley and Daphne installed themselves in the drawing room. John had taken his shaking wife back to their bedroom. Eleanor had been murmuring something about wanting to go home, and wanting to go home now. Daphne kept running through what she had seen, wincing every time she remembered Charles's eyes.

When the four of them had returned from the horror of the aviary, their sweep of the floors revealed that only Mr and Mrs Moore were in the castle: the former had been up in the attic, while Mrs Moore had been in the kitchen, sleeves rolled up as she prepared lunch.

Mrs Moore had made a pot of tea for them, positioning the vessel on a table in the drawing room alongside a tray of Kendal Mint Cake.

'Restores energy . . . after a shock,' she had said as she placed the offerings.

Once Mrs Moore had left the room, Duke leapt from Mrs Thewley's lap and began clawing affectionately at Daphne's leg. She scooped him up and cradled him in one arm whilst attempting to break off a slab of the Mint Cake with the other.

'I suggest we confer now, Miss King. Would you like to do the honours this time, or shall I?' Mrs Thewley asked.

Daphne swallowed the bite of cake and narrowed her eyes. No point keeping any cards close to her chest. Mrs Thewley had proved, time and time again, that she was one – if not several – steps ahead of her.

'You mean about young Kenneth Hammond and the fact that he appears to harbour a rather inexplicable hostility towards the man we've just found murdered outside?'

'Quite,' Mrs Thewley replied. 'Though it's not inexplicable, is it my dear Miss King? Surely your acuity has seen through the mists on that matter?'

Daphne continued to stroke the purring Duke. 'As has yours, I assume, Mrs Thewley?'

The doorbell clanged, interrupting their conference. Daphne flung Duke to the ground, offering an apology as she did so – there was no way on earth that she was going to allow the police to come and go as easily and lazily as they had done on the night of Winifred Roberts's death.

Mr Moore was striding down the hallway, but she darted out of the drawing room ahead of him.

'About bloody time,' she harrumphed as she opened the door and stood glaring at the two figures who were waiting. One, evidently the more senior of the two, was in his forties, wore a thick beard with ginger flecks running through it, and returned Daphne's glare with a pair of startlingly blue eyes. He wore a thick, navy woollen coat and removed his hat as he stepped inside. The other was a constable. He looked very green about the gills, Daphne thought. She'd be surprised if he'd even started shaving yet.

'Good morning, Miss . . . ?' the inspector said.

'Miss King. Miss Daphne King. The dead man – the man whose body is out there – his name is Charles Howton,' she spoke rapidly, for fear of wasting time.

'Inspector Forsythe, Constable Crookshank,' the inspector said. 'Mr Howton was the proprietor of Maybridge Castle, correct?'

Daphne furnished him peremptorily with the answers he sought – they were basic questions that required little thought on either side.

'Constable Crookshank and I will go and secure the scene,' Inspector Forsythe explained. 'As it appears, from your account, that Mr Howton was the victim of foul play, we'll ensure that we note down anything unusual about the scene. Then, when we're satisfied, his body will be removed. We'll require all residents of Maybridge Castle – temporary or permanent – to stay here. We'll need to ask you all some questions.'

Daphne snorted.

'Is there something ... amusing, Miss King?' the inspector asked sharply, his pen hovering about his note-book as if deliberating over whether to note down Daphne's reaction.

'I suppose there is, really. If only you'd done half of this when you were here two nights ago. Didn't have any questions for anyone then, did you, when a woman was found dead at the bottom of the stairs? Perhaps if you'd done your job properly then, the killer might not have struck again.' Daphne spat out her words.

There was a pause.

Inspector Forsythe looked at her intently. 'I'm afraid, Miss King, that I haven't the faintest idea what you're talking about. We weren't here two nights ago.'

Daphne faltered slightly. 'Well – well I suppose it was some of your colleagues then. Bloody slapdash colleagues.'

The two men looked at one another. 'Miss King, there appears to be some misunderstanding. Asperdale is a small police force. We were the only two responding officers on duty two nights ago. We received no information pertaining to a dead body here at Maybridge Castle. And we certainly weren't here at Maybridge Castle.'

Daphne's mouth fell open. Then who the bloody hell *had* arrived at Maybridge Castle two nights ago?

35

The others returned in dribs and drabs. After Eleanor's premature departure from the beach, Raymond Hammond had chosen to visit the ice-cream shop, which insisted on staying open year-round. Helena Rackham trudged back into the castle with a furrowed brow after her second stint of observing and inspecting the burial ground.

Kenneth Hammond, it was noted by both Daphne and Mrs Thewley, was nowhere to be seen yet.

All had reacted to the news with shock. Daphne made sure that it was she and she alone who told them of Charles's murder. She wanted to be the one to assess their reactions, evaluate how they responded. So far, so unexceptional. But so far, no Kenneth Hammond.

She told them also of the disturbing news that the police had no knowledge whatsoever of Winifred Roberts's death.

'How – how can that be?' Raymond asked. 'We heard

them – John spoke with them, they *took Winifred's body* with them.'

Daphne was at the mantelpiece and turned to John, asking him to describe the officers who had arrived that night. She was tossing a clove-studded orange from hand to hand, her co-ordination and ability to withstand the sharp prickling of the cloves heightened by the demands of the situation.

'Officer,' John replied.

Daphne looked at him quizzically.

'Officer, singular. One officer. Unremarkable, average height, dark hair,' John said.

The information about the officer's appearance was unhelpful, Daphne decided. It could be anyone. The news, however, that there had only been one attending officer. Now that was something.

'Forgive me for forcing you to repeat yourself, John, but for absolute clarity: there was one officer at the castle?' Daphne asked, looking over at Mrs Thewley who was nodding approvingly at her line of questioning. The orange in Daphne's hand was now being thrown back and forth with the increasing frequency of a mis-timed metronome.

'Yes, the one chap . . . I don't know . . . an inspector possibly? It was all a daze, to be perfectly frank,' John stated, shrugging.

'Then how the devil did the man haul Winifred Roberts' dead body out?' Daphne blurted.

Mrs Thewley winced. 'Miss King, a little delicacy if you please. Your passion is admirable, but there are civilians here unaccustomed to such language and such scenes.' She waved her hands towards Eleanor, Helena and Raymond.

Daphne frowned. 'Delicacy's one thing, I agree. But we're only now just learning that, firstly, one police officer attended the scene of Winifred Roberts' murder, and, secondly . . . that, well, that *no* police officers attended!'

John murmured something.

'Come again, dear Dr Beaumont?' Mrs Thewley asked encouragingly.

'He said he had another officer coming . . . someone to help . . . I was in a rush to get back to everyone, you see,' John said in a low voice. 'The whole thing – the whole thing was . . . it was too much!'

He began to cry. Daphne rolled her eyes. Mrs Thewley produced a handkerchief of unknown provenance which she offered to him.

Just as Daphne was about to offer John some choice words about being forthcoming with pertinent details, the door swung open. Kenneth Hammond.

'Where've you been, son?' Raymond asked, approaching the young man.

Kenneth was blowing on his hands to warm them, and stood near the fire in the room.

'Collecting some sea shells,' he said simply.

'Sea shells,' Mrs Thewley echoed. 'How . . . quaint.'

'Nature's trinkets, that's what Ma always called them,' Kenneth said. 'Never visit a beach without gathering some.'

Kenneth turned and smiled at them. Daphne stared at him. Was there something jovial about him? An air of content that she hadn't detected before?

His smile remained undimmed as he continued to warm his hands.

'What's all this, anyhow? Why's everyone standing around like they're at a funeral?' he asked.

Was that . . . a smirk?

Raymond Hammond's eyes darted from Daphne to his son, as if seeking approval for informing him about Charles's death. Daphne nodded.

'It's . . . Charles. He's dead, son,' Raymond said. 'Seems . . . he was murdered.'

Kenneth's smile flickered.

'Dead?' he repeated. 'Murdered?'

It was a smirk, Daphne decided. Unmistakeable. Brazen, even. Yet it then transformed into something else. She couldn't pin down the emotions that were making themselves known on Kenneth's face. Curiosity?

Disappointment? Resignation? His features eventually settled themselves into an unreadable mask, neutral and unyielding.

'Yes, dead, yes, murdered,' she said briskly. 'Several things have come to light, Kenneth. Firstly, the matter of the police officers who came to the castle after Winifred's death. Namely, the fact that there weren't any police officers here. You were the one who spoke to them on the telephone, Kenneth. Did you – notice anything unusual? Think very carefully. This is very important.'

Kenneth thought for a moment, ran his hand through his tousled hair. 'I didn't call them, Miss King, you asked me to, but it wasn't me who telephoned them.'

Daphne waited expectantly, her orange-throwing paused.

'Mr Moore did it – I was fumbling with the telephone, my hands were so sweaty I was useless.'

Mr Moore telephoned the police. A new nugget.

All were anxious to know what was going to happen now. As simply and efficiently as she could, Daphne explained the various steps that the police would be required to take. She reassured them that this Inspector Forsythe seemed a competent man, straightforward.

'We'll need to stay here, of course, as they may well want to ask further questions. And any officer worth his salt *will* ask more questions. I suggest we stick together.

Lest we forget, there's a killer somewhere in or around Maybridge Castle. A killer who has slain two people. So far.'

Helena Rackham's tea cup clattered to the table. 'T– two people?' she stammered.

What a peculiar point on which to seek clarification, Daphne thought.

'Yes, two people, Helena: first Winifred Roberts, now Charles Howton. Same murder weapon, same method. What I need to do – what the police need to do – is think about connections between Winifred and Charles. Why them? What's the link? They must have some common thread . . . something concealed that must be uncovered if we're to find the killer.' Daphne was thinking aloud now. She glanced around the table. What connected Winifred and Charles? Something from their past? Some enemy that they had both made?

As far as she knew, Winifred and Charles barely knew one another. She would need to shift her gaze. Recalculate.

The group sat in silence, each alone with their own contemplations.

Without warning, Helena began to sob.

Mrs Thewley reached across the table and patted her hand. 'There, there, Miss Rackham, it's an awful thing, I know.'

'Charles was such –' she emitted through her wailing, 'such a dear man – so kind – so full of thought and wit—'

Eleanor now also began to cry. Daphne mustn't let herself. She didn't want them to see her crying. Not if she was going to uncover one of them as the killer.

Helena went on, 'He – he didn't deserve this—'

'He didn't, Helena,' Daphne agreed. 'He was a dear friend to you, I know. He was a dear friend to me too. And I promise that I'll leave no stone unturned to find out who killed him – whoever murdered Charles and Winifred will be found, that I swear.'

This only served to amplify Helena's sobs. She was saying something, something that Daphne couldn't quite make out.

'It – it wasn't the same person, Daphne,' she blurted, her sobs now subsiding slightly. 'Don't you see – if you go down that track, you'll get yourself tied up in knots. And you might never find who murdered Charles.'

The cogs started to whir in Daphne's mind. The school motto. Ratty.

Very slowly, glancing first at Mrs Thewley, Daphne asked, 'Helena. What do you mean, exactly? How . . . how do you *know* that it wasn't the same person?'

Helena's eyes flashed wildly and she rose from her seat. 'B- because I was the one who killed Winifred Roberts.'

The entire room seemed to hold its breath. Eleanor

Beaumont stopped crying instantly and gripped her husband's hand. The Hammond men were agog, staring at Helena. John turned to Daphne and said, 'What's she talking about, Daphne? *She* killed Winifred Roberts? She barely knew the woman . . .'

'But that's not quite true. Is it – Ratty?' Daphne calmly said. '*Gloria in labore.*'

Helena had started to pace the room. 'How – how did you know?'

Daphne had only started to place Helena Rackham in her sights after the trip to Madame Marla and Madame Thelma's house. There was something queer about the Ratty episode. She couldn't quite put her finger on it at first, but she had known girls at school who had laboured beneath the weight of similar nicknames. Then there was the impassioned way in which Helena spoke of victimised women throughout history – the vehemence she had stored especially for women who were persecuted by *other* women. Then, of course, the biography. The mention of the motto. She knew that Helena and Winifred knew one another. And from what she had seen of their demeanours, she knew there was only one option for the nature of their relationship at school.

'Was she terribly cruel to you, Helena?' Daphne asked bluntly.

'Yes,' came the reply. Helena was tapping her teeth

once more. 'Mercilessly, relentlessly, *monstrously* so. Every day, for twelve years. She was a bully. Plain and simple. Made my life absolute hell. I had friends, but Winifred – she just never gave up. Day after day after day. I often fantasised about what I'd do to get my revenge. But of course I never had the guts to do anything. When I left school and went to university, I saw that life could be . . . peaceful. Could be happy. Saw that Winifred Roberts had ruined my childhood, single-handedly. I always thought: If I see you again, I'll tell you what you did to me. Tell you how happy and successful I am now,' Helena continued, the entire group entranced.

'And then, here, two nights ago . . . I did see her. And I did confront her. I told her how cruel she'd been, how my life had been a nightmare because of her. And do you know what she did?'

Daphne shook her head, although she had a pretty good guess as to how Winifred Roberts would have reacted.

'She laughed,' Helena snarled the words angrily. 'She laughed at me. Said she couldn't even remember me. Well that . . . that snapped something inside me. I wanted her to know what it felt like, to be scared, to be terrified. That game – murder in the dark. I knew what I wanted to do, I just wanted to scare her. So I followed her. Asked her again if she remembered me. Remembered the time she'd locked me in a cupboard in the science room. They'd bundled me in there, her little minions. Her cackling the whole time. Shoved me in there, locked the door. It was dark and I couldn't breathe properly. I begged them to let me out. Then I heard *her* voice. She said she knew what would cheer me up. She'd give me someone to keep me company. She opened the door just a smidge. Not enough for me to get out, but enough for her to put something in. A rat, from one of the cages in the science room. I've never been more terrified.'

Daphne shook her head in sympathy.

'How horrendous, for a poor young girl,' Mrs Thewley murmured. 'Never could abide a rat. Duke comes in handy for keeping them at bay.'

Helena continued. 'She only laughed even more. Said she *did* remember me now. Said I had been pathetic. Said I was *still* pathetic, "harping on about it", she said. Then ... I'm not proud. But I saw red. And ... I saw Charles's cane, it was lying there in the drawing room, he must have forgotten it. I saw it and I took it and I followed her and I hit her. Just the once. But once was enough.'

Helena brought her hands to her side and gripped her skirt. 'And that was that. This awful ghost from my past – was gone. Vanished. I felt ... I felt like I'd finally stood up for myself. Winifred Roberts, who had tormented me so wickedly – she was dead. I had put the past to rest.' Helena was suddenly overcome with a placid expression. As though she were finally at peace.

John Beaumont shook his head. 'But I don't understand – why are you telling us all this? Why are you standing here confessing to murder?'

Helena turned and looked at him. 'Because I could never forgive myself if Daphne or the police assumed it was one killer and therefore took their investigations on a wild goose chase. If I eluded them, then that might mean that Charles's murderer would too. And I can't have that on my conscience. Daphne – please, you must find out who killed Charles.' She stared at her beseechingly.

'You have my word,' Daphne assured her. She looked at Helena, half in pity, half in admiration. She had sacrificed herself in a bid to bring justice to Charles's killer.

The muddied waters were settling now. With Helena eliminated, Daphne felt a clarity settling within her. Tomorrow was her final day here at Maybridge Castle. And she would uncover the truth about who killed Charles. Of that she was certain.

36

Daphne had accompanied Helena outside to the aviary, where Inspector Forsythe could barely conceal his incredulity. Only a couple of hours ago, he had been ignorant about the death of Winifred Roberts. Now, he had her killer standing before him, confessing.

Constable Crookshank brought Helena to his police car. She gripped both of Daphne's hands in hers. 'Find his killer. Promise me, Daphne.'

She nodded firmly. Her doubts and suspicions had been circling, like the kite scanning for prey. Slowly, slowly, at first. Then a plunge for the kill. It was nearly time to plunge, Daphne knew it.

The inspector came into the castle and, one by one, questioned each of the guests, as well as Mr and Mrs Moore. Daphne knew what the outcome would be: nobody had seen anything, nobody had heard anything. She herself had nothing of use to offer. Try as she might, replaying the scenes in the maze, there was nothing there.

The clock in the hallway struck midday. Seven in the morning, New York time. Still too early for Veronica. Then a plan struck her. What if ... what if instead of telephoning Veronica to inform her of Charles's murder, what if she could also inform her that the culprit had been caught? That Daphne had solved it. It would be an immense load to take on, to think about – but at least Veronica would know that her cousin's killer had been apprehended.

For this, Daphne would need to accelerate the plan that had been taking shape for some time now. She would need Mrs Thewley's assistance for elements of it. And she would need the motorcycle. She would also need assurances that all the people currently under the roof of Maybridge Castle would be there when she returned on the motorcycle.

Standing in the hallway, Daphne saw Mrs Thewley approach her. 'I see you're plotting, Miss King. And I demand to know precisely what your plotting entails.'

37

The drawing room had taken on the properties and association of some kind of holding pen. None of the guests seemed at all inclined to be alone in their bedrooms, and so they sat, stood, paced or lurked in the same room in a silence that was anything but companionable.

Daphne couldn't sit down. She was restless, energised, full of momentum. Time was limited. At this hour tomorrow, she would be nearing Euston station, returning to London – never to see any of these people again. Upon hearing this in their tête-à-tête, Mrs Thewley had feigned offence – she jolly well intended on seeing her again, Miss King could bet her bottom dollar on that, as the Americans said.

The clove-studded orange had split during her hand-to-hand throwing, and had thus been written off as a casualty. Daphne had, for a time, browsed the dusty tomes lining the walls of the drawing room. Flicking through them, she found the words swimming before

her. All she could think of was the plan she had to ini-
tiate – and would have initiated sooner, had it not been
for Mrs Thewley urging a more leisurely approach.
'Let them all stew a little longer, duckie; I find some
marinading in worry and guilt does wonders,' she had
said.

Daphne happened upon a smooth piece of coral nestled on one of the shelves and was now caressing it in her
left hand. She peered at some of the Christmas cards on
the mantelpiece. Nosy, of course, to look, but she
couldn't help herself. Messages of seasonal wishes and
kindness that took on immense poignancy. Scribblings
to 'Dear old Charlie' or 'To you, you old rotter' that
wished him 'a yuletide of the usual impropriety and
japes' or hopes that 'Christmas 1936 will bring jollity
and jolly unforgettable memories.'

She could wait no longer.

She turned to the guests, exchanged a glance with Mrs
Thewley.

'Now, in case of some kind of . . . unforeseen emer-
gency calling any of us away, this Forsythe has asked me
to . . . gather everyone's addresses. Should the police
require further assistance from anyone present,' Daphne
began, deploying her most stern and school-marmish
tones. 'I have my notebook, if everyone would be so
kind as to oblige.'

She offered the book to Kenneth first, who, gripping the pen in his left hand, began to write down his address.

Mrs Thewley cleared her throat and widened her eyes as Daphne looked at her.

'Are you . . . ambidextrous, Kenneth?' Daphne asked.

The young man paused and frowned. 'Now that would be rather useful, for all those essays at university. Left hand exhausted after a few thousand words, keep going with the right hand.'

Daphne persisted. 'So . . . are you ambidextrous or not?'

Mrs Thewley tutted. Daphne knew she would be advising delicacy, but hooey to delicacy.

'Well, no, I'm not, Miss King. Rather a peculiar question to be asking, mind if you let me in on the joke?' Kenneth asked, a note of irritation in his voice.

'No joke, Kenneth, no joke at all,' Daphne replied curtly.

'Miss King, would you mind ever so assisting me in fetching my hot water bottle from upstairs? Darned knee of mine playing silly buggers, just need a little steering is all,' Mrs Thewley asked lightly.

Daphne glared at her briefly before forcing a smile and replying that of course, that would be no inconvenience whatsoever.

*

'Just because he's left-handed doesn't mean that he didn't clobber them, Mrs Thewley,' Daphne hissed as they approached the staircase, door safely closed behind them.

'No,' Mrs Thewley replied carefully, 'But it does mean that it would be far more difficult. Both Charles and Miss Roberts suffered strikes to the left side of their heads, correct?'

Daphne nodded.

'And both were struck front on, as it were? Facing their assailant? Both of them falling backwards on to the ground?' Mrs Thewley continued.

Daphne was now twiddling idly with the button on the cuff of her blouse. She nodded and muttered 'yes' sulkily.

'Which leads me – and you – to believe that the perpetrator struck both using their right hand. For Kenneth to have hit Charles with his left hand, to the left side of Charles's head . . . well, that would be a fearsome backhand that, I suspect, not even Mr Fred Perry himself would be capable of.'

'But . . . the diary . . .' Daphne began to protest.

'The diary, yes – the diary, well that does need clearing up,' Mrs Thewley replied thoughtfully. 'For the sake of . . . tying up loose ends, as it were.'

And so it was agreed. Daphne and Mrs Thewley returned to the drawing room.

*

'You're saying you think Kenneth murdered Charles?' Raymond spluttered in disbelief, sitting down in an armchair, leaning forward with his hands on his knees.

'Oh they're not picky with who they put in the frame,' Eleanor said, not unkindly. 'A sort of . . . eeny-meeny-miny-mo approach, seems to be.'

Daphne turned to her and irritably replied, 'It's a little more . . . rational than that, thank you very much. As I said, we did suspect Kenneth . . . but now we don't.'

'Crikey, lucky me. Our dynamic duo here won't be sending me to the gallows after all,' Kenneth said. 'I think I need a little snifter after this.'

'Kenneth wasn't Charles's biggest fan, I'll grant you that, but . . . murder? That's a leap too far, I'm afraid.' Raymond was shaking his head incredulously. 'Son, pour me one of those, while you're at it.'

Daphne indicated with a nod that she too was in the market for a sherry.

'It was Charles, wasn't it,' she stated baldly.

'I beg your pardon?' Raymond responded, his face blank in genuine puzzlement.

'The day your wife died. It was Charles you were sending that telegram to. While your wife drowned, you were writing to Charles,' Daphne sighed as she said this, as if deflated.

The Beaumonts looked from Daphne to Raymond, baffled.

'Wait . . . no . . . you're not saying . . . ?' Eleanor was putting some pieces together, it seemed. 'Raymond killed Charles because he was sending a telegram to Charles when his wife died?'

Mrs Thewley and Daphne both snapped 'no' as quickly as possible. Under no circumstances did Daphne want any more silt hurled into these already very muddied waters.

'Now, look here, I won't have this all being raked up . . . my wife's death . . . it's a personal matter . . .,' Raymond was saying, his glass of sherry shaking in his hands.

'And I won't have you protecting that man any longer, Pa,' Kenneth said in a surprisingly gentle tone. He turned to Daphne. 'Spot on, Miss King. I won't ask how you know. But I will say that Pa would never have laid a finger on Charles Howton. Much to my disappointment. He never blamed him for Ma's death. That burden lay with me. Charles was, well . . . a bad influence on Pa. Flighty, all over the place. Charming, of course. Debonair, a man of the world. Always turning up unannounced to try to get Pa to invest in some scheme or another. I liked him, he was . . . fun. Until, when I was twelve or so, I overheard them talking late one night.'

Kenneth swilled his sherry.

'Charles was drunk, I think. Saying he wished he'd never put pressure on Pa that day. Made him think that it was a matter of urgency to send that bloody telegram. "If only I'd known," blah blah blah.' Kenneth's words were full of venom.

'You hated him for it,' Mrs Thewley said, sadness enveloping her face. 'You still hate him for it.'

'I've tried to ... to make Kenneth ... see that ... accidents, well, accidents are terrible, but ...' Raymond was trying his best to hold back his tears as he gazed into his glass of sherry.

'If your father had been there, he might have saved your mother,' Mrs Thewley said to Kenneth. 'But then again, he might not have. Don't you think it's time to grieve your mother with sadness and love rather than with hatred and resentment?'

Daphne took a sip of her sherry. Mrs Thewley's aphorisms certainly wouldn't have been out of place in her agony column. Heartfelt yet commonplace. Mundane yet somehow ... touching.

Kenneth was looking at the old woman, the anger in his eyes softening into something else.

'Blimey, Mrs Thewley,' Eleanor piped up, dabbing a handkerchief at her eyes. 'You don't half have a way with words. She's right, you know,' she gestured to

Kenneth, 'Life's too short, isn't it John?' She squeezed her husband's hand.

Daphne frowned. This was all getting slightly too much now, as admirable as Mrs Thewley's skills were.

'Right-o, well, now we're all up to speed on that, great stuff, lovely news,' she said stridently. 'I suggest we ask Mrs Moore to furnish us with some of her luncheon delights. Keep us all occupied, at least we can discuss the flavour combinations of the cold cuts rather than sit here in silence.'

Mrs Thewley winked at her. The game was afoot. After lunch, they would take the next step in the plan they had concocted.

Daphne drove the motorcycle with more brio this time round. Time was of the essence, so she really would have to get that engine revving at least a little – or so Mrs Thewley insisted. So it was that she arrived at the antiques shop in, she wagered, half the time of yesterday's outing.

'Hallooo, Mrs Dawson? Mrs Margery Dawson?' she said in a sing-song voice.

The woman appeared from behind a stack of dusty newspapers. Today her ensemble was even more out-landish: a mink stole nestled about her neck, a black fascinator perched atop her head, and she was proudly wearing a blue and white striped pullover.

'Good afternoon, welcome to Sheep in a Bucket antiques emporium; how might I be of assistance to you today?'

Daphne explained. 'I've a rather heavy ... armoire that I should like to donate to the emporium. Perhaps you might be prevailed upon to come and assess its suitability? I've no eye for value, so it would be tremendous to have an expert evaluate its worth – see if it's something that you might like to take off my hands.'

Margery Dawson frowned and clicked her tongue against her teeth. 'Now, usually, I'd be more than happy to assist, naturally. However, I just had a telephone call telling me that a certain member of a certain royal family has heard about Sheep in a Bucket and would like to pay us a visit. All hush-hush, though, top secret and what have you. I'm to stay here and await their arrival.' Margery Dawson lowered her voice with every sentence that she uttered.

'Oh, I see.' Daphne nodded. It was a terrible lie, a blindingly obvious lie, but Daphne was operating under extreme pressure and it was the best she could pluck from her imagination when she had made the telephone call to Margery Dawson some thirty minutes ago. 'Darned dratted thing of it is, though, that I'm going on holiday tomorrow – shan't be back for another eight weeks. Jolly long holiday. And I would so hate for the armoire to be languishing in my empty house rather than proudly standing tall in your emporium.'

Margery Dawson thought for a moment.

Daphne projected her most guileless voice. 'Oh, hang on. I don't suppose – is your young man here today? Might he be able to assist?'

Margery Dawson said that yes, he most certainly was there. And that, as his employer, she had the right to send him on whatever errands she saw fit.

She rattled off to the side door that Daphne had seen yesterday. There was a low grumbling while she informed him of his afternoon task: 'eyeing up an armoire so that peculiar, clever-sounding lady out there can pocket herself – and us – a few bob.' Daphne bristled at the 'peculiar,' but admitted the accuracy of the 'clever-sounding'. Margery came trotting out, followed by the man. He had a long, narrow face, and dark eyes. Approaching Daphne, his lips appeared curled into a sneer. He was wearing a heavy work shirt and woollen trousers. He pulled a cigarette from his back pocket and lit it.

'Need a hand, do you?'

'That's right, an armoire, might be worth a bit. Can't stand the thing so I'm getting rid of it. I understand that you know your stuff?' Daphne explained.

'Oh I know my stuff, all right.' The man oozed

arrogance. Baby-faced though he was, there was something forbidding about him. 'Where we going?'

Margery Dawson made to answer, but Daphne cut in. If this was going to work, he couldn't know that she was taking him to Maybridge Castle.

'Not far – not far at all. Hop in the sidecar and we'll be there in a jiffy,' she said gaily. 'I'll even drop you back here afterwards, for your pains.'

He smirked. 'No pains. No pains at all.'

She had positively zipped through the lane on the way back to Maybridge Castle. She couldn't risk anyone leaving the castle, so it had to be done quickly.

Once there, she hoisted herself off the saddle and started skipping towards the front door before the man had even set one leg over the edge of the sidecar.

'Wait, wait,' she could hear him snarling. 'You never said we were coming here, I didn't know we were coming here—'

'Come along! Just through here!' she trilled. She could sense his disquiet. Just as she had predicted.

Reluctantly, he followed her down the hallway towards the kitchen. Mrs Moore was rolling some pastry out as Daphne entered. 'Here we are!' she said, gesturing towards the large armoire in which the wine glasses were all stored.

Easy does it, Daphne, she thought, easy does it.

She turned round to see Mrs Moore and the man eyeing each other warily. Had Mrs Moore just been mouthing something to him? She couldn't be sure. But she did know that a flash of recognition had passed between the two. All was going to plan.

38

There were only two further steps that Daphne needed to take. She had to bide her time, but it would be worth it. It was two o'clock. The group was arranged in the drawing room. Some sat, some paced. A remarkable stillness had settled upon some of the guests, while others tapped fingers or scratched ear-lobes, unable to remain motionless. Discussions had been conducted about quite what they should all do now. Charles, their host, was dead. The Beaumonts were rather keen to return to Surbiton at the earliest convenience; Eleanor was eager to put the whole ghastly business behind them. Kenneth and Raymond had had a hushed debate about whether to stay until tomorrow, as planned, or to embark upon the journey home now.

Daphne, of course, knew that she needed all the guests to remain under the roof of Maybridge Castle.

'Now, I understand that we find ourselves in unthinkable circumstances. That we none of us foresaw our weekend unfolding in quite such an awful way,' she declared in her most rousing voice. Another clove-studded orange was in her hand. She really ought to make some of these herself when she was home; inexplicably motivating prop to have about one's person. 'But Cousin Charles . . . well, he wanted us here. He sent those invitations to every single one of us. Who knows what will become of May-bridge Castle now . . . whether people will . . . whether Charles will be remembered here.' Daphne found herself moved by her own speech, despite having to improvise it as a means to an end. That end being keeping the guests where she needed them. 'I say we stay here until the bitter end. We may be the first and only guests here to know what Charles had dreamed for the place. It's the least we can do to . . . honour him.'

She clutched the orange and looked at the array of faces before her. Although confusion and anxiety remained, these emotions were now accompanied by affection, determination. It was agreed that they would stay until Monday morning, tomorrow.

After this news was communicated to the Moores, Mrs Moore offered some scones, and she was now con-ducting her rounds of the table, splashing milk in cups here and there.

'Mrs Moore,' Mrs Thewley began. 'I should very much like to discuss with you further the Van Gogh that you mentioned earlier. What with the tragedy of

Charles's death, I find myself eager to live life to its fullest, to indulge in my passions as and when I can. What say you get in touch with your man in Liverpool, ask what price he's looking for for the Van Gogh?'

Mrs Moore meekly smiled, and said that she'd be delighted to assist Mrs Thewley.

Daphne placed her tea cup in its saucer. 'I do apologise, Mrs Thewley, and do tell me to mind my own business if you wish to. But this sounds to me like a terribly precarious investment. One that I would be extremely wary about. With the greatest respect, you're a woman of advancing years – would spending a fortune on a painting really be the wisest thing to do? Let's face it, by 1940 you'll probably be as blind as a bat! As I say, with the greatest respect.'

Mrs Thewley made a harrumphing noise. Mrs Moore, in the meantime, was keeping a close eye on the interaction.

'Miss King, although you gall me . . . perhaps you're right. After all, rather sad to think of me and Duke, all alone in our pied-à-terre trying to see through the cataracts to look at the painting I spent a fortune on. And you were telling me about that cruise down the Nile – perhaps that would be a wiser source of pleasure?' Mrs Thewley concluded pensively.

At that, Daphne began painting a picture even more vivid than the Van Gogh. A picture of Mrs Thewley and Duke safely ensconced in their cabin, enjoying chilled sherry by day, perhaps joining the captain's for dinner in the evening.

The other guests chimed in as well, rendering the vision even more elaborate. And all the while, Mrs Moore watched on.

'No, he's not here. Oh, Duke, where have you got to?' Mrs Thewley was looking underneath the table. 'This really won't do – if he's gone off again, he'll be a devil to track down, and my knee's playing up once more, blasted thing.'

Mrs Thewley winced as she massaged the offending joint.

Daphne frowned, still clutching the latest clove-studded orange she had swiped from its decorative position. 'The rascal's gone walkies for, what, the seventh time today, has he?'

John Beaumont joined in the search, lifting cushions from the sofa.

'Oh, don't be so daft, Dr Beaumont,' Mrs Thewley contended. 'Excuse my bluntness, but Duke will not be nestled underneath a cushion – have you seen the size of the creature?'

There was impatience tinged with panic in Mrs Thewley's voice. Everyone noticed it. Eleanor glanced at her husband, seeking reassurance. Daphne went to Mrs Thewley and placed a hand on her arm.

'Fear not, Mrs Thewley. You have before you an expert squad of feline whisperers who will smoke out that naughty young lad before you can say, "God rest ye merry gentlemen."'

Raymond and Kenneth both rose to their feet, nodding in agreement.

'Hammond chaps – you take the upstairs,' Daphne directed, already heading to the corridor to retrieve her coat from the stand. 'Beaumonts – the ground-floor rooms. I'll head outside – I have a suspicion that our Duke might be hunting finches again.'

The maze appeared more intimidating than before. The shards of frost upon the skeletal hedges seemed poised like daggers. A bat flitted erratically in the sky overhead. She could hear a crow cawing, make out a rodent scurrying along the driveway. The gravel crunched beneath her feet. If her speculations were correct, all would be brought to light in the next few moments.

Daphne took a few more tentative steps forward. And there she was. Mrs Moore.

Before Daphne could approach the woman any closer, she was grabbed from behind and felt something cold pressed against her throat.

She was immediately struck by an instinct to fight. She began to wriggle, slamming her right arm against the figure behind her who had her fixed in such a tight grip.

'You just had to keep interfering, didn't you?' came Mr Moore's cold voice in her ear. 'Picking and prodding and nosing around everyone and everything.'

Strolling casually, as if out for an afternoon's promenade, Mrs Moore walked towards her. With venom in her voice, she echoed her husband's sentiments. 'This is your own fault, you do realise that? All you had to do was leave the old biddy alone. But no, you had to tell her not to buy that painting. You had to ruin it all. All our hard work.'

Mr Moore pressed the object closer to Daphne's throat. She knew that it must be a knife. That he had, within his power, the ability to kill her. Right this instant. Daphne had tracked crooks, met with informants in dingy pubs, foiled murderers and consorted with figures of questionable morals and, indeed, sanity. But never had she placed her own life in such immediate danger. Never had she experienced the sheer white terror of having a knife pressed against her throat.

Her hands were clammy, her breathing swift and shallow.

Get a hold of yourself, Daphne, she told herself. She focussed on the haphazard path of a bat skittering through the sky above the maze.

Focus, breathe.

'And now we have to get rid of you.'

It all happened in an instant. Mrs Moore nodded at her husband, and Mr Moore held firm while Daphne wriggled.

'Keep . . . still—' Mr Moore grunted.

Daphne kicked Mr Moore's shin, and in the momentary loosening of his grip, managed to thrust her hand into her coat pocket. She grabbed the object that she had idly, unthinkingly deposited there earlier: a clove-studded orange. With all her strength, she slammed it into the side of Mr Moore's face. He yowled, more in shock than in pain.

Daphne sprung from her position, leapt away from Mr Moore's reach, and glared at the pair.

The clove-studded orange lay on the ground. A Christmas decoration she would henceforth hold dear to her heart.

Heart pounding, slightly out of breath. Daphne said, 'Thing is – it's not just me you'll have to get rid of. It's everyone else as well.'

With that, Mrs Thewley, the Hammonds and the Beaumonts stepped out from one of the pathways in the maze.

'Thank you, Mrs Thewley,' Daphne said, 'for bringing everyone out here. Makes for jolly fascinating listening, wouldn't you agree?'

'Oh it quite does. Though I do take issue with the term "old biddy". Rather insulting,' Mrs Thewley added.

The Moores looked around in confusion.

'You didn't think you were ambushing me, did you? Oh dear. How disappointing for you,' Daphne said, tightening her coat. 'You've left such a terribly obvious trail of breadcrumbs right from word go, Mr and Mrs Moore. Though I suspect those aren't your real names, are they?'

The Moores were cornered. One shovel could not batter its way out of this.

'No, I rather suspect they have other names. That Mr and Mrs Moore are the names you adopted when you decided to connive your way into Charles's life, into Maybridge Castle. Isn't that right?' Daphne asked.

The Moores looked at one another. The game was clearly up. But Daphne could tell from their hardened expressions that the Moores were going to keep silent.

'You see, I've experienced my fair share of swindlers and charlatans in my time. They invariably suffer under the misapprehension that their intelligence exceeds that of anyone they encounter – all who cross their paths are gulls and fools. But you see, all swindlers follow the same pattern: inveigle their way into a person's life, affections. Through common interests or common values. Appealing to their weaknesses, or their passions. Earning their trust. Just as you, Mrs Moore, earned Charles's unquestioning trust when you told him about the gardener stealing from him.'

Mrs Moore narrowed her eyes. Mr Moore tightened his grip on the shovel.

'The gardener who was, of course, your own son. Because, yes, that was another lie: your son did not die under the same circumstances as Mrs Thewley's. But it's a neat trick: playing the loyal underling to Charles, a fellow bereaved mother to Mrs Thewley. Yes, as I was saying – your son. The one who now does odd jobs down at Sheep in a Bucket – as well as impersonating a police officer when necessary. Oh and the same one who was employed by Charles as a gardener – until you . . . disclosed that he was a thief. Why was it that you did that, Mrs Moore? To earn Charles's trust, I suppose. Worked like a charm, all told.'

Mrs Moore stared at her.

Daphne turned to Kenneth Hammond. 'When Mr Moore told you he was telephoning the police on the night of Winifred Roberts's death, he was, in fact, calling his son. And when your son arrived, you knew to stall. Firstly, to go and meet the 'police' when the doorbell rang. Then, to send Dr Beaumont on a wild goose chase to find pills that were somewhere else entirely. Affording you the chance to leave the drawing room again, for another period of time, supposedly to get those bloody pills. I imagine they were very easy to go and swiftly retrieve. So that you could in fact use that time to help your son carry Winifred's body out of the castle. I had assumed there were two officers. But clarification from Dr Beaumont corrected that. And confirmed a long-held motto in investigating: never make assumptions. In any case. Your son arrived, after you instructed him to come and tell whoever happened to speak with him that it was an accident, that nobody need worry. This confused me at first: it was Helena who killed Winifred, why did you need to cover it up? But of course, Winifred's murder wasn't part of your plan. It would disrupt your own plot. If the guests at Maybridge Castle thought a murder had occurred, they might not be quite so happy to hang around. Mrs Thewley might leave. And it was Mrs Thewley that you had your hearts set on,' Daphne continued. She was pacing around on the gravel, the evening growing darker.

Mrs Thewley tutted. 'What baffles me is, how on earth did you choose me?'

Daphne paused to see if either of the Moores would proffer an answer.

'Your interview in *Spiritualism Now*, Mrs Thewley. The copy that Kenneth found in the kitchen – someone had underlined several vital pieces of information. Anodyne to one for whom a criminal bent is alien. But, as I say, vital to someone adept at exploiting such titbits. You revealed rather a lot in that interview. Or rather, you revealed enough for the Moores: the death of your son; your passion for painting. Two things that they could take advantage of and use for their nefarious schemes.'

Mrs Moore shook her head. 'You don't know what you're talking about.'

'Ah, now, you bring me to my next point, Mrs Moore. On several occasions, it's been *you* who doesn't know what she's talking about. First, the stain on the curtain – you appeared bamboozled by it, when anyone with a passing knowledge in domestic tricks would know how to solve that in an instant. How could it be, I wondered, that a housekeeper with such experience could find that so troublesome? Next, the pastry fork you placed by my plate. Again, a minor detail – taken in isolation, it would be meaningless. But it was another error that I would never expect in one of your status. Then, of course, there were the other incongruities: your handkerchief, Mrs Moore, the one you lent Eleanor. I happen to be eyeing up a scarf of the same design in Liberty's – which led me to ask how did you afford such an accoutrement? And you, Mr Moore, your enthusiasm for the Balto statue in Central Park. The enthusiasm of one who has seen it in person, not just read about it in a library book. Once more: I found myself asking how a butler-cum-chauffeur-cum-ornithologist would have taken himself to New York?'

Eleanor piped up, 'But – I mean to say – people can treat themselves, buy themselves nice things? Or even travel overseas for work with their employers, that's not . . . unheard of. That doesn't make them frauds and imposters.'

'Quite right, Eleanor. All of these things, if it were just one of them, would be inconsequential. But when one observes the pattern, the patchwork of clues and things that are just ever so . . . slanted. Well, when one considers all of these things together . . . the picture forms,' Daphne explained. 'You see, I don't think Mr and Mrs Moore have ever worked in domestic service before. I think they're roles that you've inhabited. I think you've led a life of carousing and fripperies – all courtesy of the people you've swindled.'

'The great shame of this is that Charles was never supposed to be murdered,' she went on. 'He just . . . got in the way.'

'Just like you got in the way,' Mr Moore grunted. 'All he had to do was stay out of that bleedin' aviary. Time and time again, I told him. Stay out. Blamed it on the birds. Course, the birds were there, but I couldn't give a monkey's about the birds.'

Daphne nodded. 'No, the aviary was, I imagine, where you kept your . . . loot? And where you painted that very charming painting for Mrs Thewley's benefit. Yes, the blue paint flecks – one imagines you didn't have time to clear it up properly?'

It was now John Beaumont's turn to ask a question. 'But *why* did they paint it? What good did that do?'

'I'm a lonely old woman, Dr Beaumont,' Mrs

Thewley answered. 'At least, that's how I'm perceived. For Mr and Mrs Moore, the more opportunities for gaining my trust, the better. I assume that, once you had convinced me to purchase the Van Gogh, you would then volunteer to act as go-between, save me the trouble of handing the money to your imaginary Liverpudlian art dealer. I would be able to simply pass it to you?'

Mrs Moore nodded bitterly. She knew that it was all over now.

'We honestly didn't want to kill Charles. He was harmless – until he went in and saw everything in the aviary. Then . . . well, he had to go.'

'And you had taken his cane from the scene of Winifred's murder because . . . ?' Daphne asked.

'Because we didn't know then that we would have a chance to cover up the killing; taking the cane would muddy the waters, make life more difficult for an investigator,' Mr Moore explained. 'And then when Charles . . . Well, it all happened in the moment – he appeared in the aviary and I had to think on my feet. The cane was right there.'

'And to make life even more difficult for me, you decided you were going to kill me next? All because I stood between you and Mrs Thewley's money,' Daphne added.

'Jolly handy we're all here to make sure that doesn't happen,' Mrs Thewley said. Daphne smiled at her.

As she glanced in the direction of the castle, she could see two figures approaching.

'That'll be Inspector Forsythe and Constable Crookshank. If all has gone to plan, they've already picked up your son down at the Sheep in a Bucket. He'll be charged with fraud, I imagine. But as for you two – well, if only fraud were the whole of it.'

The Moores stood motionless. To run would be futile.

After the officers had taken the Moores, the guests returned to the castle. It was cold, and it was dark – but the sky was clear and Daphne stood looking at the stars. Mrs Thewley approached and placed a hand on hers. 'Well done, Miss King. Another ne'er-do-well foiled. Another crime thwarted. All because of that brain of yours.'

Daphne smiled again. That brain of hers. It would be afternoon now in New York. Time to make the telephone call.

'I'd best attempt to contact Veronica, tell her about Cousin Charles,' she sighed, full of dread.

Mrs Thewley grasped her tightly. 'It won't be easy, Daphne, but as I said to Dr Beaumont: one must have trust in the love we have for one another. Which reminds me: Duke must be ravenous. Make your call, then meet us in our chambers. I'd say a midnight feast of some sort is in order. We've missed our Sunday dinner in all this excitement.'

'That's the last of it, I'm afraid,' said Mrs Thewley as she drained the bottle of red wine into Daphne's glass. She giggled. 'Probably for the best, I'm feeling a little squiffy, I don't mind saying.'

Daphne laid down her knife and fork. She'd had two helpings of the beef Wellington and it was taking its toll on her. 'I've a nasty feeling that there's a case of the Wellington sweats coming on, Mrs Thewley. Rather rich stuff, bloody delicious though.'

'A jack of many trades, that Mrs Moore. Conniving co-conspirator and murderer by night, supremely talented cook by day. Here, any of the Stilton left? I've a dollop of chutney left on my plate that's begging to be eaten.'

Duke miaowed plaintively and attempted to swipe a morsel of beef from Daphne's plate.

'Now, now, Duke, you've had your turkey treats,' Mrs Thewley reprimanded him.

Daphne passed the cheeseboard to Mrs Thewley, depositing a chunk of Wensleydale on to her own plate as she did so.

'Now, shall we flip a coin to see which of us will sneak to the kitchen for the brandy butter and Christmas pudding, Mrs Thewley? I seem to recall there also being another bottle of Merlot in the cupboard somewhere.'

39

Christmas had come and gone. Daphne and Veronica had toasted Cousin Charles with the rest of Veronica's family at their home in Mayfair. The event had a sombre tinge to it, but all agreed that Cousin Charles would have approved of the port, the crackers, the turkey. The phrase 'here in spirit' had been uttered several times that day, and never failed to make Daphne smile.

'Oh, you're a sentimental so-and-so,' Mrs Thewley said affectionately as Daphne finished telling her about the day. 'That tough exterior fools nobody, Daphne King. Now, are you getting in, or do I have to ask your Veronica to push you in?'

Daphne was trembling on the edge of the small dock at the ladies' swimming pond on Hampstead Heath. Her teeth were chattering, and she had prevaricated for long enough: Mrs Thewley had been treading water with admirable dexterity while Daphne had stood in her towel on the side of the pond.

Veronica emerged from the changing room, impossibly elegant and unmoved by the cold. She adjusted her swimming cap, sauntered past Daphne and effortlessly dove into the pond, resurfacing beside Mrs Thewley.

'If you don't get in, then you shan't be entitled to a rewarding whiskey back at my house, and Duke will certainly think far less of you, Daphne King,' Mrs Thewley shouted as she and Veronica began to breast-stroke away from Daphne.

Whiskey and Duke's opinion of her were reason enough to take the plunge. And take the plunge Miss Daphne King did.

Acknowledgements

Immense thanks to Kate Fogg, Sania Riaz and all the team at Vintage, as well as to Laura Macdougall and Olivia Davies at United Agents. You've all helped to steer Daphne through to another adventure with care, insight and patience. Thanks also to my friends and family, for all the devilled eggs, nature's trinkets and well-chosen words they've provided me with over the years. And, finally, thanks to Rachel: without you, Daphne wouldn't still be marching around in her corduroy slacks.

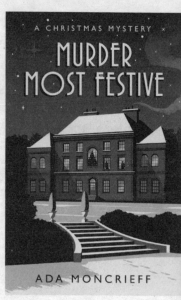